The QUEEN'S SPIES

My Story

The QUEEN'S SPIES

The Diary of Kitty Lumsden, 1583–1586

By Valerie Wilding

SCHOLASTIC

For my dear friend, Ragnhild Scamell
Always there (except when it thunders)

While the events described and some of the characters in this book may be based on actual historical events and real people, Kitty Lumsden is a fictional character, created by the author, and her diary is a work of fiction.

Scholastic Children's Books
Euston House, 24 Eversholt Street,
London, NW1 1DB, UK
A division of Scholastic Ltd
London ~ New York ~ Toronto ~ Sydney ~ Auckland
Mexico City ~ New Delhi ~ Hong Kong

Published in the UK by Scholastic Ltd, 2005

ISBN 0 439 96363 X

Printed and bound by Nørhaven Paperback A/S, Denmark
Cover image supplied by The Art Archive
Background image: Guildhall Library, Corporation of London

2 4 6 8 10 9 7 5 3 1

London, England, 1583

16th November 1583

My mother is trying to make me just like her.

"Take this book," she said. So I did. Then she suggested I keep a diary, as she does.

"Only write in it when you wish to," she told me. "Once every few weeks, if that's all you care to do. Think how pleasant it will be for your father to read of your doings when he returns from his travels."

If Father knew of all my doings, I wouldn't be allowed out until next century! I asked that if I keep a diary, could it not be private, like hers?

She smiled. "Of course it can, Kitty," she said. "You're quite right. A diary ought to be private."

I should think so! Mother began her first diary when she was my age, and has often told me how she hid it from her parents. She says she would have been in terrible trouble if they had found it, because she was rather too honest with her thoughts.

In a way, it will be nice to write down what I think. There is hardly a moment in this house when I can even hear my own thoughts!

Later

My brothers have done nothing but tease me about my diary, and I've made each of them swear never to open it. I shall tie a riband round it, with such a complicated knot that I will know if anyone dares touch it. The only one I trust is Joseph. He would never do anything to hurt anyone – especially me. He treats me like his pet, but in reality, he is mine – I try to take care of him.

So I begin my diary. But with what? All I have done today is embroider three yellow petals which Mother says resemble egg stains.

I know! I shall set down the state of our family. My father, Sir Nicholas Lumsden, is abroad, in the service of Queen Elizabeth. At least, we think he is abroad. His work is secret and he never talks about it. (So he says. But I know he talks to Mother when they are alone. She is interested in affairs of state, but that sort of thing bores me silly.)

My mother, Lady Matilda, known as Tilly, still keeps her diary. Indeed she dare not stop, for it is almost by royal order! Once, long ago, Mother performed a service for Her Majesty, who was then Princess Elizabeth. Every year, on Mother's birthday – which she shares with the Queen! – a beautifully soft, leather-bound book, marked with the royal arms, arrives from the royal court. It is a gift from the Queen, and there is always a note inside, written in HER MAJESTY'S OWN HAND, saying something like, "In remembrance of a kindness done to me by the Lady Matilda Lumsden when she was simply Tilly Middleton." Mother says she is Lady Matilda by the Queen's good grace, for she was introduced to Father by important members of the royal household.

My brother Richard is a secretary at court, but he comes home often. He is sharp and clever. His twin, my sweet Joseph, studies law at Lincoln's Inn. I fear he will be studying for a long time, as he is not as quick as the others. What he lacks in wit he makes up for in gentleness, and I love him dearly. He lodges at Lincoln's Inn, but sleeps here whenever he can. My third brother Harry goes to school, so I see him in the evenings. My little brother George is new out of dresses and into breeches. He is proud of himself and struts around taking giant men's steps! My small sister Elizabeth has called herself Beeba since she first learned to talk – which she never stops doing!

Then there is me, Catherine Anne Lumsden, aged twelve, and very happy, though I do get bored.

17th November 1583

Yesterday I forgot to mention my little dog, Pawpaw. A pawpaw is a fruit that Father once ate. It's a fitting name for my dog because when he was a puppy, his little front paws were always digging. I would say to visitors, "Watch my dog's trick." Then I would put him down and say, "Dig!" He would have dug whether I'd spoken or not, but the visitors didn't know that. Some would give me a coin to buy bones for Pawpaw. I get free bones from our kitchen. The coins bought me ribands to trim my gown!

Pawpaw is good-natured, but he has a sharp bark and would crunch the ankles of anyone who threatened me.

Today, after church, Mother asked me to take some linen to Aunt Frances. I adore her. She was Mother's best friend when they were young, and when

Frances married Mother's brother, my Uncle William Middleton, they became sisters, too.

The good thing about Uncle William is that he is the physician at the Tower of London, where I love to go. Something is always happening within its walls.

I knocked on the door, and instead of it being opened by the Middletons' maidservant Dolly, I was greeted (if you can call "Oh, 'tis you" a greeting) by my sour cousin Kathryn.

"Goodness, Kitty," she said, "look at your shoes. Did you jump in *every* puddle? How unladylike."

I did not reply, for bounding down the stairs was my cousin Edmund – my best friend in the world.

"Kitty!" he cried. "I'm off to deliver a package for Father. Coming?"

"I am sure Kitty has much to do at home," said Kathryn. "She will not want to stride round the streets with you."

A soft voice said, "Oh, I think she will."

Aunt Frances! I truly believe she remembers what it was to be young, while her daughter, though only sixteen, seems ancient.

Kathryn sniffed. "Then I will go, too."

But Aunt Frances said, "No, Kathryn, I need you here."

I handed over the linen, and followed Edmund. We wandered through the streets, shivering in the sharp wind, but I would rather be out in the cold with Edmund than sewing crooked stitches by a roaring fire.

When we had delivered the package, we ran down to the river and walked back to the Tower wharf. I never tire of the Thames, though I see it daily from my bedroom window.

I looked up at the turrets of the White Tower. "What news of the latest prisoner?" I asked.

"Tortured on the rack," replied Edmund, "but he has not confessed. Yet."

I shuddered. Although I love the Tower of London, dark things happen there. The newest prisoner is Francis Throckmorton, accused of plotting to overthrow the Queen.

I was about to ask more when I noticed a woman tottering from the direction of London Bridge.

"She's hurt," Edmund said, as she sat down. "There's blood on her skirt."

We went to help. The woman had been at a bear-baiting on the south bank, when the bear broke free. She had been hurt in the rush to escape.

"But bear-baiting has been banned since that accident in January, when the seating collapsed," I said.

“ ’Tis still popular, so it goes on,” she said, getting up. “I thank you, young lady and gentleman. Good day. And take my advice – avoid the bear-baiting.”

As if I had a choice! My mother has a strange concern for animals, and thinks bear-baiting cruel. And because of that accident, even the theatres are closed. I’ll never have a chance to see a play, either.

I left Edmund at the Tower gates, but not before we had cornered Geoffrey, a Yeoman Warder, to ask about Throckmorton.

“I can tell you nothing,” he said.

Edmund tried our usual trick. “It matters not,” he said. “We know all about his crime – it involved two Frenchwomen, a Dutch spy and a spotted dog, did it not?”

Geoffrey couldn’t resist correcting him. “No, young Edmund – he was caught writing to the Queen of Scots about a plot.”

“A plot?”

“He planned for those Frenchies to invade our country, to free her. Once she was on the throne instead of our beloved queen, the whole country would become Catholic again. But don’t worry – tomorrow he’ll be back on the rack, and he’ll talk, by God he will!”

I am sure Geoffrey is right. A few minutes being stretched on the rack is said to cause great agony.

21st November 1583

I have never seen Mary Stuart, the Queen of Scots, and am never likely to, but I feel sorry for her and fear her, at the same time. She has had a strange life – Queen of the Scots at six days old, crowned at nine months. Sent to France at five, and didn't the French love her! She married the heir to the French throne at fifteen and, by age sixteen, she was their queen, too. Her husband died two years later, and she returned to Scotland a young widow. But in the meantime, the country had become Protestant. After a rebellion, she fled from Scotland seeking Queen Elizabeth's protection from her own people.

While Mother and I got out warmer clothes – for it grows colder daily – I asked why Mary Stuart is imprisoned.

"She is a staunch Catholic," explained Mother. "Many people would like to see England return to that faith. They wish for Mary Stuart to be on the throne instead of good Queen Elizabeth. It is sensible to keep her out of sight and out of reach."

So Mary Stuart has been imprisoned in one great house after another ever since. A prisoner in England for fifteen years because she is a Catholic.

My old tutor told me about this. (I was taught until my twelfth birthday last May, as Mother insisted that I should be educated in reading, writing, some Latin – not much, I fear – and history.) Once, the whole of England was Catholic. Then the Pope in Rome wouldn't allow Henry VIII to divorce his first wife, Catherine of Aragon, and marry Queen Elizabeth's mother, Anne Boleyn. Henry was mad about Anne, so he broke away from the Catholic church and became head of the church of England. After his death, dreadful things happened in the name of God. His other daughter, Mary Tudor, remained Catholic, and when she became queen she actually burned those members of the English church, the Protestants, who refused to worship as Catholics.

Our queen has always said that as long as Catholics attend church every Sunday, and do not attempt to hear the Mass privately, no harm will come to them. Of course, they must not try to turn the rest of us Catholic, either.

"The Queen fears those Catholics who seek to put Mary Stuart on the English throne," said Mother, banging dust from my old green woollen cloak. "They would have help from Catholic countries abroad. Kitty, cut this up and make it into a cloak and kirtle for Beeba."

Oh, lovely. More sewing. Ugh! I threw Mother's fox-lined cape around my shoulders and moved from side to side, watching the heavy fabric swing. Pawpaw disappeared beneath its folds. "Being in prison for years is no way for a queen to live," I said.

Mother took a deep breath. I glanced at her in the looking glass. Her expression was cold. "While Mary lives," she said, "the Queen must constantly fear assassination. *That*, Kitty, is no way to live."

I kept quiet. Though I am all but grown up, Mother is not above boxing my ears. Mary Stuart is not worth a ringing head.

24th November 1583

It is as Geoffrey said. Francis Throckmorton has confessed. Edmund came today, with Kathryn trailing him like a pale shadow, and said the rack did its job well. They had barely fastened Throckmorton down when he began to talk. The thought of such agony was too much for him.

There will be more prisoners in the Tower soon, for Throckmorton has named those who helped him. One is Mendoza, the Spanish ambassador in London. I hope the Queen never trusted *him*.

"So the French *and* the Spanish would have invaded?" I asked.

Edmund nodded. "There would have been a huge force from both countries."

"A truly frightening thought," I said. "Imagine waking up to French ships on the Thames and streets full of bloodthirsty Spaniards!"

Kathryn squealed. "Kitty! A lady should not speak so."

But Mother clearly thought like me. "We must thank God for the clever men who discover such plots," she said. "They have truly saved England by capturing Throckmorton."

4th December 1583

Oh, I yearn for spring! Today was long, grey and dull, and all I had to occupy me was a dancing lesson, which I dislike. But everything brightened when Joseph came home, bringing an old friend.

"Look who I met!" he cried. "Sir Anthony was a student when I began my studies."

The tall, handsome young man smiled. "I fear I was a failure at law!"

Joseph laughed. "Not through lack of wits, Anthony! You never bothered to attend. You were too busy dining, drinking and gambling! And you still are."

As Mother rustled into the room, Sal, our housekeeper, brought wine to the fireside.

"Let me introduce you," said Joseph. "Madam, may I present Sir Anthony Babington. Anthony, my mother, Lady Matilda Lumsden."

Sir Anthony bowed, and said how delighted he was to have the pleasure and all that. Once Mother was seated, Joseph introduced me as "my beautiful sister, Kitty". Blockhead! But I admit I liked it when Sir

Anthony kissed my hand and said, "You are right, Joseph – your sister is a pretty Kitty!"

Mother coughed, and talk became more general. Within five minutes, she had wormed out all the details of Sir Anthony's past life. How does she do it? People tell her everything. She says listening is the art of conversation. I think speaking is. How can you have conversation without words?

At supper this evening, Sir Anthony was the main topic of all our talk.

19th December 1583

There is to be an execution tomorrow, but I have a nasty running cold and Mother will not let me go.

"You cannot walk all that way," she said.

"Then let old Tom saddle my pony for me," I begged.

"Are you mad?" Mother demanded. "On horseback! In such a great crowd!"

She is right about the crowds. There will be thousands attending the execution. The prisoner, Edward Arden, is accused of conspiring to murder the Queen. How many more are there like him and Throckmorton? It frightens me that even a queen is not safe.

I started to speak, but Mother interrupted me. "I hope you do not think to argue, Kitty."

Of course not. I would not dream of it. But I am disappointed to miss the execution. Never mind. There is another prisoner, John Somerville, who was arrested for shouting against Protestants and the Queen as he ran through the streets. He was thrown in the Tower before he knew what was happening, and will soon be executed. I'll be better by then.

20th December 1583

Kathryn brought me one of Uncle William's horrible concoctions. "It will ease your cold," she said.

I examined the potion. There were *things* floating in it. "My cold is better, I thank you."

Kathryn looked down her beaky nose. "Then what is that green crust on your upper lip?" she demanded.

Mother said quietly, "Drink the potion, Kitty."

"Yes, Madam," I replied. "I'll take it upstairs and sip it slowly."

Kathryn barred my way. "That is precisely what my father said you would do."

Mother sighed. "Drink it here, Kitty," she said, "then Kathryn can be on her way. I am sure she has much to occupy her at home."

"Indeed I do," said Kathryn as I downed the potion in three swallows. It was revolting. I made a great show of trying not to be sick, and was very satisfied to see Kathryn jump aside, just in case. I cannot bear her. She likes to show me up at every opportunity.

There was a loud bang on the door. Sal and Edmund burst into the room.

"Welcome!" I cried. "Have—"

Kathryn interrupted. "Brother, your visit is fortunate. You may accompany me home."

"Can Edmund not stay?" asked Mother.

"Indeed not, Aunt," said Kathryn. "He must study. He needs much knowledge if he is ever to be apprenticed to our father."

Edmund made a face behind her back. Then he said, "I'd like to show Kitty a puppy I saw playing along the road. May I, Aunt?"

"A gentle stroll will not harm her, if she wraps herself warmly," said Mother. "It will give me a chance to ask Kathryn's advice about a difficult colour in our new embroidery. She is such a good needlewoman."

Kathryn looked smug, but I didn't care. I grabbed my cloak, and we were gone.

There was no puppy at all – it was a ruse to get me out! I was disappointed that Edmund did not have news of the execution, but he was not allowed to go. He did, though, have some interesting news from the Tower. John Somerville, the madman who shouted against the Queen, was taken to Newgate prison yesterday and was found this morning, strangled in his cell!

"Who did it?" I asked.

"The Tower is full of men who are loyal to the Queen, silly," he said. "Any one might have done it, but I doubt if there will be much attempt to discover the murderer. You know what will happen next?"

"What?"

"Somerville's head will be chopped off and taken to the gatehouse on London Bridge. It will be boiled, then covered in tar to stop it rotting."

"Ugh!" Having been forced to try boiled pig's head at last year's Christmas feast, I could think of nothing nastier. But that is the purpose of putting traitors' heads on spikes on the bridge – so all who enter the city can see the penalty for treason and be disgusted. And afraid.

We had just decided to follow a drunken beggar to see what would befall him as he reached the river when Kathryn appeared.

"Ed-*mund*!" she warbled. "*What* are you doing? And Kitty, stop behaving like a street urchin. Go inside and keep warm. I'll be back tomorrow with another dose."

When she turned her back, I stuck out my tongue and waggled my fingers like donkey ears. Edmund saw and spluttered, earning a sharp look from his sister.

It is a pity Somerville was murdered. Now there will be no execution. Not that I wish to watch a man die, but an execution is such a good reason for an outing.

24th December 1583

I have been bad-tempered today, for we are fasting in preparation for Christmas Day. Mother allowed us only bread and some very tired apples. I feel full of lumps and cannot wait for the feast after church tomorrow.

11th January 1584

Sir Anthony Babington has visited our house three times in as many weeks. He entertains Joseph with other friends in his lodgings or in taverns at least twice a week. Joseph says he can afford to be generous.

"Is your friend rich?" asked Harry over dinner.

"He is," said Joseph, "though it is none of your business." He turned to Mother. "Sir Anthony has a thousand a year."

Mother smiled. "A good sum! He is fortunate. No wonder he lost interest in his studies. George! Elbow off the table."

Beeba grabbed George's knife and I took it from her before she sliced her fingers off, then sat her on my lap.

"Anthony Babington is from Derbyshire, is he not?" asked Mother.

How does she know?

"His family home is there," agreed Joseph. "Poor man, his father died when he was ten."

Oh, *stop,* I wanted to say. Couldn't we talk about anything else? Joseph has been to the theatre, and I want to hear about it. I was so excited when he said the theatres are open again. The Queen has formed a company and they are to play every day except Sundays. Wonderful news!

But no. They wanted to talk about Babington.

"Anthony served as a page in the Earl of Shrewsbury's household," Joseph announced as the maids cleared away.

"Oh?" said Mother sharply. "Kitty, let us work on our embroidery while Joseph amuses us."

He will amuse me as much as watching Pawpaw's legs twitch in his sleep, I thought. And the embroidery is the bane of my life – a wall-hanging of unicorns and fair ladies and about a *million* flowers, and we stitch it together. Mother says I am so slow that it should be finished by the time I marry, so I may have it. I do not want it.

I closed my mind to Anthony Babington, and invented a story in my head about a great nobleman whose life I saved. He presented me at court, and rewarded me with ponies and a basket of snow-white kittens. I was just about to become the Queen's closest, most trusted friend when I was startled by a loud banging at the door.

Sal hurried in. "'Twas the court messenger, My Lady," she puffed. "Sir Francis Walsingham is coming!"

Mother leapt up, shooting scissors and needles all over me. "Kitty! Bestir yourself!"

I groaned. Sir Francis is so *dreary*.

12th January 1584

Thankfully, Sir Francis did not stay long, otherwise I would have spent hours in my bedchamber, with just candles for company.

He and Mother (and Father, of course) are friends, but his visits are not like those of others. Often, as last night, we must keep out of the way while they talk. I have no idea what they speak about. Our walls are too thick. Normally, if you polish a doorknob for long enough, you're sure to hear something interesting, sooner or later, but not from Sir Francis. His voice is low, and you only ever hear odd words, like "majesty" and "privy council" and "Catholic" and "insurrection", whatever that is. It sounds deadly dull to me.

20th January 1584

Richard visited today – the first time since Christmas! He is no more handsome than his twin, but his court clothes are so fine that poor Joseph seems but a pale copy. We drank sweet spiced wine, which made me hiccup, while he told us the court news. It was dull stuff. I want to know things like does Her Majesty sleep in a golden bed (he does not know), and is she like a fairy queen (he snorts).

Mother is interested in court affairs, so the rest of us sat stupefied, the wine and fire making us hotter and sleepier, while Richard rambled on. One thing intrigued me, about the Spanish ambassador, Mendoza, who plotted with Throckmorton to put Mary Stuart on the throne. They didn't execute him.

Instead they expelled him from England. He left yesterday, and good riddance, I say. Richard said Spain will simply send him somewhere else, where he'll carry on plotting.

"Throckmorton will not be as lucky," Richard continued. "His guilt is clear. And it was treason."

I shivered. The punishment for treason is death. And execution can be quick and merciful, or slow and agonizing.

25th January 1584

Mother rode off to visit friends, with old Tom attending her. She said I might spend the day with Edmund, if Aunt Frances didn't mind. She never minds anything! The only minding in that household is done by her pompous daughter. Sure enough, as soon as I arrived, Kathryn was on at me – pick, pickety, pick.

"How unladylike!" she snapped, when I belched by mistake. "Hold this." She passed me the huge cloud of greasy sheep's wool she was preparing for spinning. (Spinning! Oh, it turns my brain to fluff.)

"Where is Edmund?" I asked.

Kathryn looped up a strand of frizzy ginger hair that had dared to come loose. "In his chamber, at his Latin books," she said. "So you may as well help me. When we have finished, I'll show you the cover I am making for my prayer book."

"I'd love to see it," I said, and I hope God will forgive me for the lie.

I don't know if He'll forgive me for what happened next, for what did I see? Edmund, outside, making faces at me through the window! Come outside, his lips said. Suddenly he ducked down. I turned to see Aunt Frances, looking at the very spot where he'd been.

"Er, Kathryn," she said, "could you spare Kitty to run back home to borrow a ... er ... to borrow your aunt's, er..."

"Red kerchief!" I said quickly. "She said you like it."

Aunt Frances smiled. "The red kerchief."

Kathryn sniffed. "I suppose I can manage."

"I'm sure you can," I said. "You spin so ... so... "

"Deftly," Aunt Frances said helpfully. She saw me out. "Have fun," she whispered. I love Aunt Frances.

Edmund and I were attracted by shouting from the north side of the Tower, at the Royal Mint, where they make our coins. We ran to see what was happening.

Two workers were quarrelling. One swore that the other had deliberately dropped a hammer on his foot, and he'd nearly fallen in the ash pit. Even from outside the mint I learned some words I've never heard before! Edmund clapped his hands over my ears. I chased him back across the green, but the Raven Master stopped us and accused us of frightening his birds. Hah! It would take a lot more than me to frighten those great ugly black creatures. When Beeba was tiny, Mother wouldn't allow her within the Tower walls in case a raven mistook her bright dark eyes for something tasty.

Oh, I adore wandering round with Edmund. The smallest things are fun.

8th February 1584

Richard sneaked in quietly today, to surprise us. He caught me with my diary. "Are you writing about your string of lovers, Kitty?" he asked. "May I see?"

I ran to my bedchamber and hid my diary behind a loose wall panel. I've made a vow. My diary will never, ever leave my room. Here it is safe.

18th February 1584

Joseph brought two friends home today, and Mother invited them to supper. One was Sir Anthony Babington, and the other was his friend, Chidiock Tichborne.

Mother asked Sir Anthony about his time in the Earl of Shrewsbury's household.

He laughed. "Sheffield Castle was strange. The Earl

lived in one part with his family, and in another, separate section, was a special prisoner."

"Oh?" said Mother. "Who was that?"

Sir Anthony put down his bread. "None other than Mary Stuart, Queen of Scots," he said, with an air of importance.

"Indeed?" said Mother.

"She had her own servants," said Sir Anthony, "but occasionally I would wait upon her with messages from the Earl and so forth."

Mother asked, "And what did you think of the lady?"

Sir Anthony smiled. "She is beautiful and kind. She thinks of others constantly and puts up with conditions unsuited to a queen."

"Without grumbling?" I asked.

"Well ... she does grumble," said Sir Anthony. "To be truthful, she is an expert grumbler!"

We laughed.

"She complains constantly!" he continued. "But don't blame her. Her life has been difficult. Her future is bleak."

He proceeded to go on and on about Mary Stuart, so much so that I began to wonder if he was not half in love with her.

As for Master Tichborne, he said little and seemed ill at ease, but I did not dislike him.

13th March 1584

I have had nothing special to write about for an age, but today Father came home! He cannot stay long, but it will be lovely to sit and hear him talk – not that he tells us much. It's all, "We rode here, we rode there, the weather was fine or foul". If I ask what he did, he says, "My duty, little Kitty, and that is all you need to know."

14th March 1584

Father is tired this morning. He and Mother lay long abed. I hope his work does not bring him into danger. I accidentally overheard him telling Mother of threats from France and Spain. Could this be to do with Mary Stuart and her secret supporters? Is that where Father has been?

Eventually I grew cold sitting on the floor beside their door, and went downstairs. There I found Edmund who had come to invite me to an archery contest! Kathryn was going to the shoemakers so, if we were careful, we would have a whole day without her.

I sent Edmund to ask Father, and he shouted through the door: "Uncle! May I take Kitty to the archery contest at Smith Field?"

"Good morrow, nephew!" Father called. "You may take her if you swear to look after her as if she were your sister!"

"I swear, sir!" He made a face. Kathryn needs little looking after. It would be a brave thief who tried to rob *her*!

We followed the river until we were level with St Paul's Church. It's not the quickest way, but it is lively with street sellers, beggars, sailors and children playing. Then we walked north to Smith Field. The streets were crowded with people heading the same way. We began to run, afraid we wouldn't be able to see for thousands of spectators.

And there were thousands. *And* we could hardly see.

But it didn't matter. Shooting arrows is shooting arrows the world over. I've seen it before. We contented ourselves with watching whatever was going on around us. Edmund bought some hot codlings, but the apples must have been old when they were baked. Instead of bursting from their skins, they were shrivelled, and woolly inside.

"One day I'll win a prize here, Kitty," Edmund boasted.

"Against the rest of London?" I dodged a very wobbly stilt walker. "Don't forget, every man can shoot, even Harry, and George must start to learn this year, by law, for he's almost seven now."

Edmund laughed. "The Queen need have no fear for her safety if George is protecting her! Come, Kitty, let's see what sport we can find in the streets."

As we wandered home we shared a hot meat pie Edmund bought from a little round woman whose tray was so laden, it was a wonder she could walk.

What he said about the Queen's safety made me think of Mary Stuart. "Edmund," I said, "do you think we should fear the Scottish queen?"

He laughed scornfully. "Most certainly. Although it's not the woman herself we should fear, but her supporters and their many plots."

"Many?"

"Oh yes. Time and again prisoners are brought to the Tower, suspected of treason. Mary Stuart's name is often on their lips when they confess. I know, because Father attends those who have been racked."

I shuddered. Uncle William is gloomy enough as it is. To think of him in a dark, damp, stone cell with blood on his hands makes my skin crawl.

15th April 1584

It's been such fun having Father home. My other uncles and their wives and children have been to stay, one family for ten days, and the other for nearly two weeks! I'm glad our house is large enough for all these people. Edmund's house has barely enough room for his family.

Mother and Father have entertained most evenings, and I have often been allowed to stay up playing cards with the grown-ups. I have spent whole days playing with the little ones and telling them stories.

The best thing has been having new clothes made! Father brought Mother several rolls of embroidered silks, and a length of deep butter-yellow satin for me. We spent hours choosing ribands and trimmings. My yellow gown will be the grandest I have ever owned. I'll need new shoes, too. None I have are suitable. Or, as Mother puts it, none are fit to be seen.

Edmund came today to join us in saying farewell to Father, who is off on his travels again. Kathryn would not venture out in the fine drizzle, but she sent a leaving gift for Father – a kerchief she has embroidered. It has orange roses on it!

Old Tom had a hard job holding the horses. They tossed their heads and danced, eager to be away. Father was less eager. He held Mother close, and I saw her shoulders shake. Then he clasped the boys' hands, and Edmund's, and finally kissed me and Beeba. I cried. I think my tears upset Father, because he turned away. I was most satisfied when he pulled out Kathryn's kerchief and blew his nose upon it.

In moments, he had turned the corner and was lost to sight for – who knows? Weeks? Months? We all went inside and did whatever made us feel better. Beeba cuddled the wooden doll Father gave her. Harry went outside and kicked his leather ball against an oak tree. Joseph and Richard, who had come to say goodbye, disappeared to talk dull talk. Mother scolded the cook, who'd given Beeba the most disgusting curdled milk for breakfast. And me? I sat and cried, and Edmund sat with his arm touching mine, not speaking. I liked that.

23rd April 1584

Poor Harry came home from school almost in tears today. He forgot to take his penknife with him this morning, so could not sharpen his quill. He borrowed another boy's knife, and cut himself. The master gave him two blows across the knuckles: one for being forgetful and the other for being careless. Mother bandaged the ink-stained cut and asked me to take him to Uncle William, but Harry nearly lost his head at that thought. I'm not surprised. Some of the things Uncle William puts on cuts and sore places sting so badly, you would rather have two cuts instead.

It's a pity Harry would not go to Uncle William's – I should have been able to snatch a few minutes with Edmund. I heard Richard say he suspects Sir Francis Throckmorton might be executed soon, and I wish to know if it is so.

27th April 1584

Surely the skies must soon be empty of rain. It has poured for three days! The wind is so strong and the streets so muddy that Mother has forbidden me to leave the house. It must be dangerous upon the river. Boats have been abandoned, and the streets are dense with carts and wagons. Everyone is bad-tempered and blames everyone else for the crush.

I am bad-tempered also, for I hate being cooped up like one of our chickens, and if I see one more frayed hem, I will scream.

But I soon forgot needles and thread when Edmund arrived with news. "Kitty," he began. "You know how I detest school?"

I do. Edmund is always in trouble. He has a quick tongue and is frequently beaten for insolence, though I am sure he doesn't mean it.

"Never mind," I said. "School's over for today. Come and sit with me."

We settled on the window seat overlooking the street. Pawpaw jumped into my lap and stared at Edmund. It is a habit he has. Most people find it disconcerting, but Edmund was too excited to notice.

"Father is to take on a second apprentice!" he announced.

That was not the most thrilling news I've ever heard, but I pretended to be astounded. "Well!" I said. "Goodness gracious!"

Pawpaw jumped down and nibbled my duck-egg blue slipper. I pulled my foot away, teasing him, and he nibbled again.

"Kitty, listen!" said Edmund. "Who do you think the new apprentice will be?"

I shrugged.

"It will be your cousin, you ass! Me!"

"You!"

He looked affronted. "I am quite capable of becoming a physician."

"When did Uncle William tell you?" I asked.

Edmund nibbled his lip. "He hasn't exactly told me, but—"

The door opened, and Kathryn sidled into the room. "There you are, brother," she said. "You should have come straight home. Good day, Kitty."

She's so sly. The wretched girl follows Edmund everywhere.

"Come," said Kathryn. At the door, she put on her muddy pattens and tottered down the path. Edmund whispered, "Come with us, Kitty. You will hear Father's answer as soon as I do."

"I cannot." Mother had ridden out with old Tom to visit a sick friend, so I could not ask permission. Edmund promised to come straight back to tell me.

When Mother did return, she was furious about the teeth marks in my blue slippers.

28th April 1584

Edmund did not return, so this afternoon I begged Mother to let me visit the Middletons.

"Put your pattens on, then," she said. "I don't want another pair of shoes ruined."

Ugh. I hate pattens. They make me walk as if I have no knees. I fastened the ugly lumps of wood to my feet and stomped to the Tower. Pawpaw ran beside me, his tummy skimming the mud.

Dolly let me in, and helped me remove the pattens. She took Pawpaw to the kitchen and I went in search of Edmund. Kathryn and Aunt Frances were out, so I knocked on Uncle William's study door and went in.

The stink! Some nasty mixture was being boiled up and I swear the steam was green. I don't look too closely around his study. There are dried bits of plants and animals in jars, and white bones that I shudder to think of.

Uncle William greeted me and returned to his work.

"Where is your newest apprentice?" I asked brightly.

"How did you know?" he asked. "Ah, Edmund told you, I suppose. Well, he begins studying with me in three weeks' time."

"Why not before?" I wondered.

"He will not arrive until three weeks have passed."

"But he's here already, Uncle William."

He paused. "Ah. Edmund has not told you that I turned down his request."

Oh, poor Edmund. That is why he did not return. He was probably too upset.

Uncle William said Edmund needs more schooling yet. "He may not wish to be a physician, Kitty. He may wish to be a lawyer, or find some position at court. He is lucky to be able to choose. I had no such choice at his age. My future was decided for me by my father."

That was it. Uncle William droned on and on about the bad old days. How he walked miles to school, and miles home again, trudging through deep snow. (Didn't the sun *ever* shine in the bad old days?) How he started work in the dark and finished in the dark. Truly, I have heard it all before.

Luckily, Uncle William's hideous green potion boiled over. He completely forgot about me and I was able to escape. I let myself out of the house, rather than disturb Dolly.

Did my ears ache when Mother saw me! *Where* were my pattens? *Look* at my skirt! *Look* at my feet! *How* were those shoes ever to be cleaned? On and on she went. I began to think I'd rather listen to Uncle William.

The worst thing was that Kathryn called later, bringing Pawpaw back. I had forgotten my darling little dog! That awful girl looked so smug, and when Mother said I'm not fit to be the poor creature's mistress, she positively smirked.

26th May 1584

Such excitement! Well, it is terrible, but Edmund is certainly excited. We had been visiting the Middletons, and he asked my mother if we might stroll about for a while.

"Stay around the Tower," said Mother.

We decided to go down to the wharf, which is certainly "around" one side of the Tower. Almost instantly, we found a dead cat washed up by the tide. It was in good condition, so we did what we always do when we find a dead animal – we took it to the Royal Menagerie. You get in free if you take something to feed to the lions. The menagerie is outside the main walls, but is still part of the Tower. We were about to go in when there was a commotion at the main gate. We ran to see what was happening.

Uncle William's new apprentice was being carried home. And he was dead! He'd slipped in front of a carriage, and a horse reared and stamped on his head. The poor boy had been with Uncle William for barely a week!

There was such a fuss! In the middle of it, Mother appeared and swept me away, but not before Edmund whispered, "Do you realize what this means?"

I do.

27th May 1584

Edmund came first thing today before school. I was in my chamber, but he threw pebbles at my window until I looked out. I ran down to let him in.

"Kitty," he said. "Do you think I should ask Father again? About being his apprentice?"

"Of course," I told him, but a voice behind me said, "Hold on."

It was Joseph, getting ready to take Harry to school.

"Edmund," he said, "the boy is scarcely dead, and your father must still be shocked. Wait until things are calm. In the meantime, help him all you can."

He turned to me. "Kitty, Beeba is standing at the top of the stairs in a puddle. Call someone to clear it up."

"Yes, Joseph," I said. "See you later, Edmund."

4th June 1584

Today Edmund will ask Uncle William if he can begin his apprenticeship. I am bursting to know the answer.

Later

I cannot believe it! Uncle William has agreed to take Edmund as his apprentice, but has extracted two promises from him. First, he must devote himself to becoming a good physician. Easy – Edmund is clever, and he knows lots already from watching his father. Second, Edmund must continue to read Latin and French for an hour a day. He will not do that, I know.

5th June 1584

Edmund and I are going to suggest to our parents that we read French and Latin together, to encourage each other! One day we can read at his house, the next at mine. We can even read in the garden. Or as we stroll by the river. We won't mention the garden and the river just yet.

7th June 1584

They have agreed! Edmund and I may study together!

Mother said, "Your father may think differently, but I am in favour of you learning all you can. And Edmund, I am sure, can teach you much."

I don't know that that is so.

19th June 1584

It is not as I expected. I have hardly seen Edmund, and we have not yet read together. Mother says he needs a few days to settle down, and will soon develop a pattern of work and study. A few days!

24th June 1584

Mother was right. Edmund and I have met for the last three days in each other's houses, and we have studied our books. Actually, we talked more than studied, but who will know the difference?

We plan to escape outside sometimes, when everyone – especially Kathryn – thinks we are studying.

2nd July 1584

Today I lost Pawpaw! There was nobody at home except the maids, and Edmund was with Uncle William, tending a prisoner. Prisoner, hah! What about me? What about Pawpaw?

I tried to remember when I'd last seen him, but I couldn't. I searched the garden first, in the shrubs, among the fruit bushes, and in the onion patch. The gardeners hadn't seen him, but they are half asleep most of the time.

Next, I walked along the street, calling him. Then, as I turned into Watergate, I heard someone call my own name.

It was Anthony Babington, with a friend. "Sir Anthony!" I cried, and burst into tears.

"Come, pretty Kitty," he said kindly. "Why so sad?"

When I explained about Pawpaw, he told me to stop worrying. "There are three of us now to find him. Eh, Robert?" he said.

"We started the day with nothing to occupy us," said his friend. "Now we have a quest!"

I feared Pawpaw might have gone to the river, so we went in that direction. "Suppose he gets on a boat and is taken out to sea?" I said. "And suppose the boat's captured by pirates, but suppose they have a cat and they don't want a dog, and suppose they maroon Pawpaw on a desert island..."

The two men looked at me oddly. Sir Anthony's lips twitched. "You have a great imagination, pretty Kitty."

We combed the river bank, searching among the cranes and warehouses. Suddenly I heard a sharp yap.

"Pawpaw!" I shrieked.

He was on the back end of a boat. When he saw me, he leapt into the water. But there were boats everywhere and I was sure he would be hit, and drowned.

"Holy Mother!" Sir Anthony breathed in a sort of prayer. "Save the poor creature."

Pawpaw swam this way and that, his legs beating the water. Then brave Anthony Babington waded towards him – but Pawpaw disappeared beneath the surface. I screamed! Sir Anthony stretched out, almost overbalancing and, at last, he snatched my little dog to safety.

I burst into tears again when the sopping bundle was put in my arms. I couldn't stop thanking Sir Anthony all the way back to my house. I put Pawpaw down. "I cannot ask you in," I said, "as my parents are not at home. But I will never forget your bravery, Sir Anthony."

He laughed. "I am glad your little dog is safe. Now I must return to my lodgings. My breeches and hose are no longer fit for London society! Come, Robert."

Robert took my hand to say goodbye, and I am ashamed to say that Pawpaw immediately bit his ankle.

"Forgive him!" I cried, as Robert danced away from him. "He does not know you, and fears you might harm me." I scooped Pawpaw up and scolded him.

Robert forced a smile. "He does not know me," he said, "but he knows what I taste like."

Anthony laughed and led him away.

As I dried my darling dog before the kitchen fire, my mind ran over what had just happened. I remembered Sir Anthony seeing the danger Pawpaw was in, and saying, "Holy Mother!" That is something I would never hear in my own home. For the Holy Mother is the Virgin Mary, and Roman Catholics pray to her in their prayer beginning, "Hail Mary…" I do not know the rest of the words.

But I do know now that Sir Anthony Babington is a Catholic.

8th July 1584

At last! Francis Throckmorton, who threatened the very life of Queen Elizabeth, is to die. The execution will be at Tyburn.

"Madam, will you go?" I asked Mother.

"You know I will not," she answered.

Aunt Frances has told me of the executions she and Mother witnessed when they were girls in the Tower. Mother, of course, being a good listener like me, also heard much about the torture of prisoners from her father and Uncle William. Consequently she no longer has the stomach for the spectacle of an execution.

"There will be a great crowd going to Tyburn," she continued. "The streets will not be safe for a young girl alone."

Damnation! (That's a new word I learned from Richard, which I must teach Edmund.) I was bending over my sewing, so Mother couldn't see how cross I was, when she said, "But Joseph will take you."

I leapt up, scattering silks on the floor. "May Edmund come, too?"

Mother smiled. "If Joseph is agreeable."

Of course he is agreeable. Joseph does anything I ask. I just hope we can escape Kathryn.

11th July 1584

I slept so deeply last night that my maid had to drag the covers from me this morning. When I opened my eyes, the sun almost blinded me.

"I can see nothing but yellow blobs now!" I complained.

Anne grunted. "You will see nothing but stars if your mother finds you still abed. You are to go into the city with her."

"Oh, I hope we will ride," I said. "My legs ache so."

"You are unlucky," said Anne gleefully. "Lady Tilly says it's perfect walking weather."

So it is not until this evening that I am able to escape with a candle and write about yesterday. The day a man died for his evil plot.

When Joseph and I called for Edmund, he slipped out, quickly pulling the door closed behind him.

"Hurry!" he said. "Kath—"

Too late. That witch yanked the door open. "Have you forgotten, brother, that I am coming?" she snapped. "Joseph, give me your arm."

Sweet Joseph. He smiled down at her as if she was the loveliest girl in the world, instead of a nasty, sour-lipped, stuffy rat-in-petticoats.

We set off along Great Tower Street, and were not too early, for many apprentices were already on their way to Tyburn. They had been given the day off by their masters. Everyone wanted to go. It's not every day you watch the execution of a man who plotted against the Queen.

By the time we reached Gracechurch Street, the way was busy indeed. It had rained during the night and the cobbles were slippery with mud, horse dung, and other rubbish.

Kathryn fussed and skipped to avoid dirtying her shoes. She must have driven Joseph mad with her demands to move here, cross there, but he never showed it. We met with a flock of sheep on their way to market, and it satisfied me greatly when a moist, grass-stained mouth nibbled the back of Kathryn's skirt.

We passed Newgate prison, went down High Holborn and into the Oxford road. The crowds were thick, and I kept hold of Edmund's sleeve. Kathryn took all Joseph's attention. "Hold me, cousin," she cried in her supposedly dainty voice, which I think is a weasel's squeak.

We could get nowhere near the gallows, but we knew we would see Throckmorton when he was strung up, for he was to be hanged, disembowelled and quartered.

As we waited, I smelled gingerbread, which I can never resist, and Joseph bought us each a piece. Kathryn turned her nose up at it – but in such a ladylike manner – and said she would not eat it, because the woman who sold it was filthy. I thought of her sheep-stained skirt and enjoyed my gingerbread.

Great cheers and shouts told us the prisoner was near!

"He will have his last drink at the inn round the corner," said Joseph.

Soon the crowds parted as horses carved a path through them, but we could see nothing until the execution party climbed on to the scaffold. There was lots of talk, which we could not hear, then the crowd hushed as Throckmorton made his final speech. I was shocked to see how young he was – not above 30. Then Kathryn started complaining about the crush and the smell, and saying she wanted to go home. She twittered so much, I never heard a word of the rest of the speech.

The noose was placed over Throckmorton's head and – he was dropped. He lashed out with his feet, kicking the air, and the crowd was silent. When he stilled, he was cut down, either unconscious or dead. Only those close by could see what happened next. They let out a great "Aaah!" and Edmund said that was the disembowelling. Ugh.

Kathryn immediately spoiled everything by pretending to faint. I know she was faking because she went "Aaah," twice, because Joseph didn't hear the first time. Then she slumped against him.

"Come," said Joseph, picking her up. "We must take Kathryn home."

Edmund was as furious as I as we fought our way through the crush. Once free of the crowd, Joseph puffed, "It is too far for me to carry her. I will pay a carter to take us. Hey!"

In no time, Kathryn was sitting in the back of a cart with Joseph, looking most disgruntled. Perhaps she imagined herself being carried home like a princess in a handsome knight's arms. Hah! On second thoughts, she does not have that much imagination. She probably hoped Joseph would hire a litter, or a white palfrey, to take her home.

"We'll follow," called Edmund, and Joseph threw him a coin.

"Feed Kitty," he said. "She must be starving!"

Indeed I was! As we walked we made a meal of two hot pies with the most delicious gravy, and some fresh warm bread (which, as I write, still sits in my stomach like a cannonball).

Mother flicked my bodice when we arrived home. "I see you have eaten well," she said.

I had gravy drips down my front. "Sorry, Madam," I said, "but I am not the only dirty one." I told her about the sheep, and she laughed.

"Gravy will be easier to clean than grass," she said. "Go to it."

15th July 1584

Richard visited with news. William, the Prince of Orange, has been assassinated! It is believed the Spanish arranged his murder. He was a Protestant, in charge of some people in the Netherlands who were rebelling against their Spanish rulers.

"So now William the Silent is silent for ever," said Richard.

The Prince was called "Silent" because he was good at keeping secrets. Like me. Kitty the Silent.

Richard thinks the Queen should send some soldiers to help the Protestant rebels fight the Spanish. But I doubt if she'll take any notice of what he thinks. She has dozens of advisers, and probably listens most to her favourites, like Sir Francis.

16th July 1584

Lord, I am so BORED. Kathryn is ill, and I must spend my days keeping her company, trying to lift her spirits. Kathryn's spirits are, to my mind, dreary at the best of times and harder to lift than a barrel of ale.

Yesterday, I began with good heart. I smoothed her pillow and brushed her hair off her forehead, though it is so wiry, it simply bounces back. But when I fanned her face with the flowers I'd brought, she complained that they dropped greenfly on her so would I please do the sensible thing and put them in water.

Honestly! What do you *do* with Kathryn? Uncle William gives her medicine, Aunt Frances feeds her – all I can do is entertain her.

I tried reading, but I stumbled over too many words, so she told me to stop. Then I tried telling her a story, but she said my head is full of fanciful nonsense. So I sat by the window and sang at the top of my voice. I am not tuneful, so it must have been painful to Kathryn's delicate ears. I hope so.

Somehow I do not think she is as ill as she makes out.

17th July 1584

Another day in Kathryn's stuffy bedchamber. I discovered that she was supposed to be going to Chelsea to help her aunt with a newborn baby. She is probably pretending to be ill so she doesn't have to go. That is nasty.

19th July 1584

I am so cross! It's early on a golden summer morning, with scarcely a breeze. Joseph and his friends are planning an excursion across the river with a basket of food and wine, and I must sit with Kathryn. The day will be so dreary, I can hardly drag myself out of bed.

Last night, at supper, I learned something that made me wish I hadn't been horrible about Kathryn not wanting to go to the country. For now it's my turn. We are going to Father's brother for part of July and the *whole* of August!

Fortunately, we won't be in a village like Chelsea. We will stay in a fine house, where there will be feasts and music and dancing.

20th July 1584

Yesterday evening, as Mother and I sat sewing in the little parlour, we heard Joseph and his friends talking and laughing in the next room about their river outing.

Mother said, "Poor Kitty. You will miss Edmund while we are away."

I shrugged. "I will miss all the happenings in the Tower, certainly," I said, "but I hardly see Edmund these days. He's busy with Uncle William, and I sit with Kathryn. He never visits her room."

Mother smiled. "I suppose not."

After another burst of laughter from the next room, I said, "I will miss Joseph more."

"Yes," said Mother. "He brightens up the house. His friends, too."

I nodded. "Especially Sir Anthony Babington. He makes me laugh, and I will never forget how he saved Pawpaw."

I hesitated. "Mother, I believe Sir Anthony is a Catholic."

She didn't speak for a moment. Then she said, "There is no law against being a Catholic."

"I thought there was."

"No," she said – abruptly, I thought. "Let's hope tomorrow is your last day of keeping Kathryn company. You must be slightly weary of her."

Slightly!

I ran out of thread. When I opened the closet to get more, the conversation in the next room grew louder, and I heard, "...could hardly get back in the boat for laughing..." It was as clear as if the speaker was in the room with us.

Mother smiled. "Close the closet door, for pity's sake! We don't want to hear any more of that."

I'd have liked to. But I obeyed, and the room was quiet again, except for the snip-snip of Mother's scissors as she undid a messy piece of work (mine).

21st July 1584

I knew that stuffed, pasty lump of a girl was faking! Aunt Frances had a message that Kathryn was no longer needed in Chelsea, and suddenly we have a *miracle* cure. She's up and about and snappy and pickety as ever. My hair is untidy, my skin is dull, I sit badly. Not a single word of thanks for giving up my *life* for these last days.

But Aunt Frances was full of hugs and whispered thanks. I expect she would much rather have me as a daughter than Kathryn.

When I was *finally* allowed home, I saw old Tom taking a familiar horse to the stable. I ran inside and gave Richard a hug. He's so handsome in his court clothes.

"I hear you have been comforting our cousin," he said.

He well knows what I think of Kathryn! Before I could think of a reply that was fit for Mother's ears, there was a burst of noise and Joseph came in with his friends.

Richard clasped hands with Joseph and I marvelled, as I often do, how two men, so alike, can be so different. There was a round of introductions, and Richard said, "Sir Anthony and I are already acquainted, at court."

Sir Anthony beamed. "I have seen you often, Master Lumsden. Your skills are much admired."

Richard inclined his head. "As I'm sure are yours."

Sir Anthony laughed. "I have no skills! I am good for very little."

"Not so," said Joseph. "There are many who are glad to have you for a friend. You cheer all our days!"

"And I am glad to have you, too, Joseph," said Sir Anthony. "And your lovely family. You are a lucky man."

Sir Anthony is far away from his mother and his home. Perhaps he thinks of us as a new family!

Once the young men were supplied with ale, Richard, Mother and I moved away to the window seat.

"I'm surprised to see Babington here," said Richard. "You know he is from an old Catholic family?"

Mother smiled. "I know he is Catholic. But all my sons' friends are welcome here, as you well know. And I am old enough," she continued, "to remember a time when it was dangerous *not* to be Catholic."

She meant when the Queen's sister, Bloody Mary Tudor, ruled England.

"In confidence, Madam," said Richard, "there are changes coming. Soon I believe it will not only be treason to be a priest, but also that those who help or shelter priests will face death."

"Sir Anthony is no priest," said Mother. "Like everyone else, he must attend church or pay a £20 fine. As long as he does not hear the Catholic Mass, he commits no crime."

Richard did not argue, simply saying, "Joseph must take care."

We all fear for Joseph at times. Because he is so trusting, he is wide open to trickery. But I think he will not suffer at Anthony Babington's hands.

24th July 1584

We have spent the last three days preparing for our journey to the country. Pawpaw senses I am going away and fears I will leave him here, which I must. Mother says travelling with a dog is a nuisance. Old Tom will care for him. I cannot help crying every time I look at him. Pawpaw, I mean, not old Tom.

3rd September 1584

Home! Back in my own chamber with my own things. Back to writing in my diary, which has been safe in its hiding place behind the wall panel.

Pawpaw nearly exploded when he saw me. I was even pleased to see Sal, until she began grumbling about the state of my clothes. For goodness' sake – I have been in the country!

But I have made such a mess of my apple-green shoes, playing football with my cousins, that as soon as I got home I took them outside and tossed them deep into the currant bushes. I will pretend that I left them in the country if Mother asks.

I've missed Edmund so much. Tomorrow I will visit the Middletons with the gifts we have brought, and perhaps I can see him.

4th September 1584

We had an unexpected visitor just as I was leaving for the Tower. A court messenger arrived to say that Sir Francis Walsingham was on his way.

Mother looked confused. "I wonder why," she murmured, as the maids rushed round making everything ready.

We soon found out. He had brought Mother's birthday diary.

"I shall be away for a few days, my dear Tilly," he said, "so I took the opportunity, as I'm passing, to deliver Her Majesty's birthday gift myself." He handed her the usual leather-bound book filled with thick creamy paper.

Mother didn't ask where Sir Francis was going. That's because he keeps everything he does secret. He knows all that goes on, Richard says, both at court and elsewhere. Sir Francis the Silent. Only he is not *always* silent. He talks to both my parents. Mother says Sir Francis feels he can be himself in our house, because we are loyalists. Or did she say royalists? Loyalists, royalists. They are the same.

I suppose Sir Francis must spy on people to get to know all he knows. But he cannot spy on everyone. He must have others to help him. More spies.

16th September 1584

Since we returned home, Edmund has come to study only once. Uncle William keeps him too busy. Joseph wonders at me being so desperate to bury myself in Latin. Bless his simple heart! Edmund and I just open our books in case someone comes upon us, and talk to our hearts' content.

29th September 1584

Poor Joseph! He was walking down a lane last week, and came upon an elderly man in a dreadful state.

Joseph offered help, and the man said that unless he had seven shillings by midday, he would be thrown out of his lodgings; his sick wife, too.

Joseph, being Joseph, immediately handed over seven shillings, and the man promised to meet him in that same spot a week later, when he would repay the money.

Today was that day. Joseph went this morning and we were horrified when he arrived home just before midday, pale and bleeding. Once we had calmed him down, he told us what had happened.

He'd reached the corner of the lane, by an alley, and waited for the elderly man. Before long, there was a shout of "Ho, there!" from down the alley.

Joseph turned, recognized the man and started towards him. Suddenly, two more men appeared – huge ones. They pounced on Joseph and, seconds later, they were gone! Those beasts robbed my gentle brother of his doublet, money, and a ring given him by our grandfather. It was all a wicked plot.

Joseph's face was cut and his knuckles were raw where they'd scraped against the wall. Mother was gentle with him as she cleaned his wounds. She has told him time and again not to be so trusting, but he never learns.

1st October 1584

As I read to Mother this evening, Richard came in, threw himself down before the fire and tickled my ankles. I kicked him.

"Ow!" he said. "And here I am to tell you that you shall have the pleasure of my company for a few days. I am not needed at court." He made to get up. "But if you kick me away..."

I laughed. "Stay. You make a good footrest."

"What news from court?" Mother asked.

"Not much," he replied. "The talk is all of how Mary of Scotland is being sent to Tutbury Castle, in Staffordshire. She will have a new gaoler, Sir Amyas Paulet."

"I know of him," said Mother. "He is a loyal servant of Queen Elizabeth. But what of Tutbury? Is it pleasant?"

"I fear not," said Joseph. "Damp and cold is all that can be said of it."

"Why must she move?" I asked.

"For security," said Richard. "If she stays too long

in one place, there's a danger of her worming her way into the affections of local servants, and perhaps getting their help to free her."

"Can she not be sent back to Scotland?"

Richard laughed. "She would not thank you for that, Kitty! She is no more welcome there than here. And it's unlikely that our queen would put another queen in danger – her own cousin, too."

"It must be a nuisance for the Queen having to keep Mary Stuart prisoner," I said. "Perhaps she could be banished from England and go abroad. Then all would be well."

Mother frowned. "Kitty, do not forget that Catholic countries, like Spain, would like nothing better than to restore the Catholic religion to England. And what better way to do that than to put a Catholic queen on the throne?"

My heart jolted when I realized her meaning. Freedom for Mary would mean Queen Elizabeth must die.

2nd October 1584

Joseph's spirits are back to normal, thank goodness. At least his judgement seems to be right about his friends. Anthony Babington, for one. He brings small gifts to Mother – flowers, sweetmeats – and he plays with Pawpaw, and is always giving dinner to Joseph and his other friends.

The autumn sun is warm, so when Edmund turned up with his Latin books, we went into the garden. Kathryn had followed him, of course, but Mother kept her chatting.

Hearing the clatter of hooves, we went to see who it was. I expected Richard, but it was Sir Anthony, come to cheer Joseph after his encounter with the thieves. They joined us in the garden and Joseph called for Sal to bring ale. Edmund and I took up our books, so it would look as if we were studying.

The men chatted and I listened. When everything went quiet, I put down my book and said, "I hear that Mary of Scotland is to change prisons."

They stared.

"It is true," I said.

Joseph looked bemused, but Sir Anthony seemed to be interested – or pretended to be. "Do you know where she is to move to?" he asked.

I said Tutbury. His face hardened. "The poor lady will be uncomfortable there," he said. "Tutbury is a cold, gloomy place."

"You remember her well?" I asked.

"I will never forget her," he said. "She is brave, strong and true to her faith."

And yours, I thought.

He stood, looking past me. "Lady Tilly," he said.

We all got up. I don't know if Mother heard me talking about Mary. If so, it could not have mattered, as all she said was, "Kitty, Edmund, to your books."

18th October 1584

We dined with the Middletons after church today. When we had finished, Aunt Frances took Mother into her little garden to ask her advice about some herb or other. Kathryn trailed behind them.

Richard, Joseph and Uncle William gathered round the fire. Edmund and I sat watching the little ones and listening to the talk, which was all about the prisoners Uncle William – and Edmund! – have attended. The Tower seems full of traitors. Catholic priests, too. One was in fetters for over six weeks, before being put in Skevington's irons, which is a torture instrument. It squeezes the prisoner's body so hard that blood comes out of his ears.

"Let's hope," said Uncle William, "that the Bond of Association will put an end to Catholic attempts to usurp its true monarch." He raised his glass. "Her Majesty's health."

I mouthed to Edmund, "Bond of Association?"

He shrugged.

29th October 1584

I am such a ninny. When I threw my green shoes into the currant bushes, I forgot about autumn. Now the leaves have fallen and Mother has found them.

I blamed Pawpaw. "You *naughty* dog, you should be whipped."

Mother glared at me. I felt as if "I did it," was written on my heart.

"Dogs!" I said.

30th November 1584

I have been so busy. Poor Mother slipped in the muddy edge of our pond and fell, twisting her ankle. She can't move around, and relies on me to check the maids' work, see that Sal keeps the cook in order, and check that Lucy looks after the little ones properly.

Luckily, Mother can do *lots* of sewing, which has set me free from my needles.

Today Uncle William said she might try walking. She said how lucky she is to have him to treat her. Uncle William likes to be praised. It doesn't matter what you say – you can never overdo it.

"I wish, Tilly," he said, "that I could be an ordinary doctor. But I dare not suggest leaving the Tower. I fear the Queen's displeasure."

"Oh, Uncle," I said, "surely she would understand. And who knows, suppose you treated someone famous, and suppose the Queen heard of your amazing healing powers, and suppose she summoned you to court and one day you saved her life! You would become her personal physician for ever!"

Uncle William smiled (a rare thing). "Thank you, Kitty. Why not come over tomorrow and spend time with Edmund? You scarcely see him these days outside of study times."

Aha! Flattery is a wonderful thing.

1st December 1584

I had two glorious hours with Edmund this morning. I was well wrapped in my thickest cloak, so we wandered round the Tower, chatting and throwing scraps at the ravens. Of course, when the Raven Master appeared, we pretended we were throwing scraps *to* the ravens.

Edmund has found out about the Bond of Association, which I had forgotten. It is fearsome. It calls for death to anyone who plots against Queen Elizabeth. That's fair and just. But it also insists on death for anyone who is the cause of the plot, whether they have anything to do with it or not. So if a group of Catholics planned to kill the Queen in order to put Mary on the throne, not only would they be executed, but Mary could be, too! This is so even if she didn't know what was happening, or if she disapproved! Thousands have signed the Bond, and every one of those signatures is the name of a man who has sworn to defend the Queen and rid the land of those who plot against her.

Last night Joseph stayed with some friends, and brought them all home at midday to dine with us. There were five: Anthony Babington, Tichborne, Robert Barnwell (the man who Pawpaw bit), Charles Tilney and Henry Dunn. They all looked as if they hadn't slept.

Mother muttered about Joseph living too wild a life, and that he neglects his studies. "He does not have a fortune like Sir Anthony," she said. "He must make his way in the world, and needs to study."

She is right. My brother must work harder than most. Learning is so difficult for him, he cannot afford to waste time.

I told Joseph about our uncle wanting to leave the Tower and asked, "Do you not think the Queen would be understanding?"

"I'm sure she would," he said.

Sir Anthony disagreed. "The Queen does not like to be rejected," he said. "She can be unforgiving and impatient with people around her, and she changes like the wind."

"Is that not how a queen must seem to behave?" I asked.

He paused. "In my opinion, a queen should be gentle and patient. For instance, in Shrewsbury's household, the talk among the servants was of the thoughtfulness and concern that the Queen of Scots showed to all, from the highest to the lowest. She was a prisoner, remember. That, to me, is queenly behaviour."

After a short silence, Mother hobbled from the room. I think she took praise for the Catholic queen as criticism of Queen Elizabeth, and I think Sir Anthony was wrong to speak so. But I was Kitty the Silent.

19th December 1584

Father is home!

23rd December 1584

I overheard Father telling Richard, Joseph and Mother that England must never think of herself as safe. There are constant threats from abroad. Richard agreed, and said that Sir Francis Walsingham is glad of all the information that reaches him.

I think Sir Francis has spies in France and Spain, and many other places, so he always knows what foreigners are planning, and can foil their schemes.

Richard knows a lot about Sir Francis's doings.

7th January 1585

Our Twelfth Night revels were great fun, and I am too tired and heavy-headed to get up this morning. I wore my newest gown. It is the colour of lavender, and the stomacher is embroidered in dove grey. It is not bright, but it is very grown-up. Even Kathryn complimented me on it, but she picked on my dancing all evening, and once called my behaviour "coarse". I think Mother would have slapped her if her own mother hadn't whisked her from our sight.

Later

In spite of heavy snow, several people called today, bearing little gifts and thanking us for last night's entertainment. Sir Anthony Babington brought beautiful flowers. I don't know where he got them at this season – perhaps from some hothouse. There is little in our garden but holly berries.

While he was here, Kathryn plodded in on pattens, and was introduced to him. He was charming, as ever, though he surely thinks her as dull as I do.

9th January 1585

The snow has cleared and Father is off on his travels again – he says it will not be for long. Poor Edmund has a fever! I went to see him, and said that as soon as he is well, we must go sliding in the snow on Tower

Hill. Kathryn tutted at my "childish ideas", but I was Kitty the Silent and ignored her. Then she said how impressed she was with Sir Anthony Babington. "A true gentleman."

"Really?" said Edmund.

"Oh yes," she said. "I always know a true gentleman when I meet one. His manners impressed me greatly."

Lucky old Sir Anthony.

11th January 1585

Edmund is better, but the snow is melting. I am furious. I wanted to go sliding, and now I cannot even go walking because of the slush. Worse, Kathryn haunts our house like a whey-faced ghost. She seems to wish for my company. Or Mother's. I cannot tell which.

15th January 1585

Now I know why Kathryn haunts us. Sir Anthony was here today, and Kathryn could not take her eyes from him, nor stop giggling. I believe she has a passion for him!

18th January 1585

Today, Joseph told me Sir Anthony is going abroad with some friends, visiting France and Italy, and who knows where else. Joseph is upset not to be part of the company. He has always considered himself a close friend of Sir Anthony.

"Joseph, my sweet," I said, "Sir Anthony is probably conscious that your studies are important. He would not wish to tempt you away from them."

He nodded. "It would be like him to think of my

future," he said, adding, "I fear Kathryn will be saddened by Anthony's departure. Will you tell her?"

"Gladly!" I said. That will wipe the simpering smile off her face.

21st January 1585

I think I preferred the simpering smile. Kathryn is bad-tempered and pickety, and is again doing her best to get Edmund and me into trouble. Thank goodness Aunt Frances can handle her. She listens to Kathryn's complaints, nods, tuts and says she will speak to my mother about it.

Edmund and I must find a way to get together without Kathryn knowing.

23rd January 1585

Ohhhhhh! That *Kathryn*! She drives me to distraction. If we are at Edmund's house, she's there. If he comes here, she follows him. Go *away*!

30th January 1585

Sir Francis Walsingham visited – again. We are conveniently between the palace at Greenwich and the other palaces further upriver. Sometimes he calls while he waits for the tide to turn, or when he's on his way home to Barn Elms, west of London. Today he brought good news! Father will be home for a short while next month, and Sir Francis promises that when he has been to court and given his reports, he may spend lots of time with us.

Sir Francis took his usual seat by the great fire. Mother suggested I might like to amuse myself in the little parlour, which meant, "Go away, Kitty".

I took up the rotten embroidery. With the closet door open, and my stool pulled in as far as possible, I could hear all that was said. Most of it was tedious, about people I've never heard of. But then Sir Francis mentioned that Mary Stuart is well established at Tutbury, and that Sir Amyas does a good job of ensuring the lady behaves.

That means ensuring she can't escape. I am relieved. I know now that should Mary ever be free, Queen Elizabeth would be in mortal danger, and Spain might invade England.

One sad thing is that Mary is not allowed letters from friends. The only ones she has are from the French ambassador in London, which must be deadly dull. How awful never to hear news of anyone. I hear news from Edmund, Joseph and Richard, and even from Sir Francis himself, if he did but know it!

Also, Mary is not allowed out without her gaolers, and she may not give money to the house servants, in case they are bribed to help her. Even her laundresses are forbidden to pass beyond the Tutbury walls.

I drifted into a daydream. If this were my prison, I'd find a way to escape. I'd plait all the silks and wools in our cupboard into a long rope and climb from the window. Or I might signal to a passing ship, and a handsome sailor would rescue me at midnight. I might disguise myself…

I had no chance to think of a disguise, for in burst Harry!

"Why are you in the closet?" he demanded.

"I'm not," I replied.

"You are."

"Maybe I am, but it is only to save getting up for silks, and besides, the open door protects me from draughts."

"Come and play," Harry begged. He was carrying his peashooter, so I refused. He only wanted a target.

Luckily, Mother called me to bid farewell to Sir Francis. Edmund must have been watching, for he appeared seconds after Sir Francis and his servant turned towards the river and their waiting barge. He came indoors and played cards with Harry and me. Once Harry had lost more counters than he cared to, he went to the kitchen to beg a morsel of food, and Edmund and I could talk.

"Where's your sly sister?" I asked.

"Bathing herself," he said.

"In this weather?" I said. "She must be mad."

He grinned. "She reached up to a shelf for a pan of stew that Dolly had left to cool. Guess what happened!"

"Stew on her head?" I was delighted!

"So," said Edmund, "I can tell you my news in peace."

His news was that a man called Gervase Pierpoint has been released from the Tower and banished from the land. Edmund isn't sure why he was imprisoned – something to do with him being Catholic, so perhaps he was trying to spread the religion. I found this of little interest, and wondered why Edmund even bothered to remember it. Then he told me Pierpoint was the first prisoner he ever attended with Uncle William.

Edmund cannot understand why it matters what Catholics do, so I told him what a threat they are to the Queen. He was quite interested in Mary Stuart when I talked about her wanting to escape, and about the foreign armies who might help her. But when I said it's sad that she has no letters, he lost interest. No heart, that boy.

Next he told me about another Edmund – Edmund Neville, in the Tower accused of plotting to murder Queen Elizabeth. And he is not alone. There are others. Even the Earl of Arundel is imprisoned for writing traitorous letters.

So serious threats to the Queen do not only come from abroad. Some have started very close to her indeed. It seems she cannot even trust her own nobles.

2nd February 1585

Late last night I stared out over the river, imagining the horror if we were ever invaded, and Spanish boats swarmed up the Thames.

Joseph came to say goodnight. He had been drinking – a lot – in a tavern with his friends. Even though Sir Anthony is away, Joseph still goes out too much, and spends too little time studying. Father will be displeased.

However, I was glad to talk. We sat against the pillows, my quilt around our shoulders, and I spilled out my fears of Spanish boats, and one queen cruelly murdered while another rides through the night to claim her bloodstained throne.

He laughed, and said my imagination is like a young colt – skittering and bouncing all over the place.

"Don't you worry about Mary Stuart's supporters?" I asked. "Suppose they did manage to free her? Suppose they did kill the Queen and claim her throne? We Protestants would be in danger, would we not? Like when Bloody Mary reigned." I had another terrible thought. "And it would be doubly dangerous for our family. The Queen gives Mother a gift every year... Sir Francis visits us... Father works for the Queen... Richard works at court... We would all be thrown into the Tower."

He smoothed my hair back. "Sweet Kitty, do not worry. It will all seem better in the morning."

Whoever marries Joseph won't have the brightest, most successful husband in the land, but she will surely have the kindest.

3rd February 1585

Joseph told Mother about my night worries. I'm not sure I like that. Next time, I will ask him to keep my words to himself. He must be like me, Kitty the Silent.

But I do feel better, because Mother called me into her chamber today while she was putting away some jewels.

I curtsied. "Madam?"

She held out her arms. "Come, Kitty!"

We embraced, then she said, "Joseph told me you fear a Catholic uprising. You must not. There are good, clever men watching over our queen and country. I know it."

I know she knows, because I hear her talking to Sir Francis. He's one of those men. And I believe Father is, too.

Then Mother told me that steps are being taken to ensure a Catholic rebellion will never happen. "Mary Stuart's followers will find it impossible to risk conspiring against the Queen," she said.

I think she means the Bond of Association is to become law, and all I can say is thank goodness.

15th February 1585

Edmund and I are sick of Kathryn following us everywhere. Today, after our studying (in reality, we played dice in a store room on the top floor), we strolled to the river and, in seconds, there she was! She must have been watching for us to come out.

We were pleasant, but I kept a frosty face. I don't want to encourage her. She walked beside us, watching me constantly, and it was, "Your mother wouldn't like you jumping on and off walls, Kitty..." or "Kitty, keep away from cranes, they're dangerous..." or "Kitty, *leave* that filthy cat alone..."

We must work something out.

23rd February 1585

The whole household is in a panic, for a message has reached us that Father may be home *tonight*! We have dusted, scrubbed, tidied and baked – well, the servants have. I helped Mother make herself look beautiful, and Joseph helped Lucy occupy the little ones.

I'll stay awake until Father comes. How good to have him safely home.

24th February 1585

I fell asleep! But it did not matter – Father woke me himself first thing this morning. He rode through the night (from Dover, I believe) and demanded to see his children before collapsing in bed. Now we all creep round like mice.

Later

More turmoil! We are going to the country for a few weeks. Father is tired. He says he needs to feel England wrapped around him, and to live quietly, free from the pressures of court. The Queen has permitted him to leave London, and we are to spend the spring at Winchester, in my grandparents' home. They will be pleased to see their son, but I remember that they do not care for children. Father says Winchester city is lively, with a vast cathedral. I hope it has shops and a market. Otherwise it will be deadly dull.

I do not want to go, but I only need see the shadows beneath Father's eyes to know that he needs rest. I wish I did not have to leave Pawpaw, though.

28th April 1585

When I am grown up, I will never leave London. We've been away for nine weeks! Oh, how good it is to be in my own bedchamber, away from my grandparents' stuffy house, and all those fields and forests. Winchester was pleasant, but once you had seen it, you had seen it.

Pawpaw ignored me when he saw me first. I believe he is fonder of old Tom now than he is of me. But Edmund was glad to see me. He says I missed an execution in March, of a man named William Parry who came into the country, planning to murder the Queen. Some say the Pope in Rome was behind the plot. That's not surprising. The Pope said long ago that if a Catholic kills the Queen, it will not be a sin, as she is a heretic (*he* says) because she does not believe in the Catholic faith. Of course she does not.

Edmund is full of his knowledge. But I discovered that he didn't see the execution. Parry was executed at Old Palace Yard in Westminster, and not at the Tower. I wonder if the Queen watched it. How does she feel when someone who wished her dead is put to death? I would feel glad.

But it makes me think. "See?" I told Joseph, "More plotters. We are not safe in our beds."

He smiled. "Silly Kitty. The very fact of Parry's execution should reassure you. He was caught."

"*He* was." I went to the window and looked out over the river. "But, Joseph, how many more killers are out there?"

"The Bond of Association is now a law of the land," he said. "It must put off any would-be plotters."

If that was supposed to make me feel better, it didn't. Joseph is such an innocent. Even though he spends his time with lawyers, I sometimes think *I* know more than he does. That makes me worry for him. He is low in spirits, too. Mother frequently asks if he has letters from Sir Anthony or his other friends abroad, but he does not. He is forgotten while they have fun in Rome, or wherever. That is bad of them.

14th May 1585

Such excitement! Mother was sitting on a bench beside the fountain, and I was sprawled on the grass, making a daisy chain for Beeba and watching George gallop round on his hobby horse. Suddenly Edmund flung open the gate in the back wall of our garden, crying, "Kitty! Come!"

"Whatever's wrong?" said Mother.

"The Queen!" he gasped. "Coming upriver. May Kitty come and see?"

"Of course! Hurry, Kitty! Take the little ones – they would like to see their sovereign, too."

Edmund clutched Beeba's hand tightly, and I dragged George along. Already a crowd was forming as people hurried down the narrow lanes leading to the river.

We, of course, could go on the Tower wharf, so Edmund carried Beeba and we raced through the Bulwark Gate, down to the riverside.

Not a moment too soon! The royal barge swept up the river, the tide helping the oarsmen in their work.

As it neared us, the bells of St Peter's, the Tower church, rang out, and between the dings and dongs we heard music coming from the barge itself.

Such a glorious sight! Draped in green and gold, the Queen's barge had huge garlands of flowers at the front and back (or fore and aft, as Edmund Cleversticks put it). There were no oarsmen aboard; all the rowing was done on a smaller boat tied in front. That one jerked in time with the rowing, but the royal barge glided smoothly through the water.

As it drew level with the Tower there was a mighty explosion! Then another! Beeba screamed and George buried his head in my skirts.

"It's only the Tower cannon, greeting Her Majesty," laughed Edmund.

My ears rang! I kept my eyes fixed on the barge, which now drew level with us. I could see the Queen clearly through the glass window of her cabin. She stared straight ahead.

"Why does she not look round?" I wondered.

"It's said that she hates the Tower," said Edmund.

Of course. Her mother was executed there and, as a princess, she was herself imprisoned in the Tower. It must hold bad memories.

I gazed at the small figure until the barge slid past

and I could no longer see her. How strange that so much revolves around one woman. How terrible that so many wish her dead. I shivered. Looking around at the cheering crowds, it was consoling to realize how many love her.

Edmund took us home, and I told Mother what we had seen. "You should have come," I said.

She smiled. "I have no need to. I have special memories of Her Majesty."

She has, too. Mother once did something quite unladylike in order to meet the Queen. I don't know what it was, but it would probably shock Kathryn far more than my running about with my skirts flying.

4th June 1585

As Mother and I finished cutting dead flowers off the rose bushes a sudden thought made me giggle.

"How strange my Winchester grandparents would find our garden," I said. "If they were to sit here and close their eyes..." I giggled again.

Mother looked amused. "What?" She closed her eyes. "I hear Beeba nagging Pawpaw … bees humming … boatmen's shouts … ah! They would be surprised to hear the roars of lions!" She smiled. "I have not been in the menagerie for years."

"Would you like to go?" I asked.

Her eyes sparkled. "Why not? Shall we? Lucy can watch the little ones."

So we did! It was probably not the best day for the menagerie. Everything smelled so vile in the heat. After we'd tired of the leopards, lions and wolf, and had seen the prickly porcupine, we called on Aunt Frances, who wrinkled her nose.

Mother laughed. "Frances! You look just as my mother did years ago when I tried to sneak indoors after going to the menagerie!"

It's nice to think of Mother as a girl.

I saw Edmund briefly when he came to collect a dose of something revolting for the Lieutenant of the Tower's stomach. If I were treating someone as important as him, I would at least make it taste nice.

I wish every day was like this.

18th June 1585

I'm glad I had that lovely day with Mother, for I've been ill ever since. I have had a cough, spots, a dripping nose, my throat has been raw and my ears feel as if someone's fists are inside pushing to get out. Mother has fed me thin broth, and Joseph gives me red wine, and I've swallowed concoction after concoction that Edmund has brought. I swear that boy's as bad as his father. He would not let me pretend to drink the medicine. I had to drain every drop, and there were bits floating in it. Ugh!

Worst of all, Kathryn visits me daily. She amuses herself with her so-perfect tapestry while I sleep, and reads aloud from the Bible when I'm awake. Oh, she drones on so! I asked her to make up a story instead but she's absolutely unable to. No imagination. So I made my own daydream. She probably thought I smiled because of her beautiful reading of the Psalms when, in my mind, I galloped on a cream palfrey, trying to escape a knight clad in black. Far away, beyond a shining lake, was the glint of silver armour and the flash of a snow-white cloak. Ride, Kitty, ride for your life!

21st June 1585

I am spotty and tired, but I have no pasty Kathryn today. She is accompanying Aunt Frances on a visit to her grandmother, who is staying in London.

Father visited me this morning. He wore his travelling clothes.

"Don't look sad, Kitty," he said. "It's for a few days at most. Sir Francis and I are going into the country to conduct some business."

I knew it! Father does work for Sir Francis. Is he a spy?

"I told Edmund to take care of you while you are out together, but Kathryn said I needn't worry. She will look after you both." He winked.

I groaned. "Father, she never leaves us alone!"

"Then you must be cleverer than her, mustn't you." He kissed me and was gone. But where?

When Joseph visited me, I challenged him. "What does Father do?"

"He works for the Queen, you know that."

"But what does he do?"

"I don't know exactly," said Joseph, "but I'm sure it's important. He's friends with high people, like—"

"Sir Francis. And what is Sir Francis's business? Spying!"

"Kitty you are fanciful. Sir Francis is the Queen's secretary of state – far too busy to lurk in dark corners, spying on people."

Inwardly I am seething. How can Joseph be so stupid? If Father is a spy, then he is in danger every day of his life.

Oh, I'm so tired of my own thoughts. Where is Edmund?

23rd June 1585

I feel cross that I had to ask for Edmund to visit me. But he came as soon as he could, and we had a happy afternoon playing cards. I told him I think Father is a spy, and he laughed.

"Your daydreams get sillier and sillier, Kitty!"

I've only myself to blame for that remark. In the

past I have shared my daydreams with Edmund, and now I wish I hadn't.

25th June 1585

Today I was finally allowed out for a walk. I took Beeba, George and Pawpaw to the Tower, to give Aunt Frances some of Mother's gooseberry preserves. We've too much from last year, and the gooseberries will soon be ripening again.

While we were there, a Yeoman Warder came and asked Uncle William to attend a prisoner urgently. When my uncle returned, he sat down heavily and told Aunt Frances, "Sir Henry Percy's dead. Killed himself. Three shots in the chest."

"Shh, William." She indicated the children playing marbles on the floor. "Why?"

"He was accused of plotting against the Queen," he whispered, but I heard because I moved closer. "If he'd been executed, all his lands and titles would have been given to the Crown."

"The Queen, you mean?"

"In a way. They wouldn't be hers, personally – she'd have to pass them on to whoever becomes king or queen after her. Anyway, it doesn't matter. Percy cheated the law by killing himself first."

It's a dangerous business, wishing harm on Her Majesty. Now I'm hot and bothered, because hearing of plots and conspiracies stirs my fears.

11th July 1585

Mother and I were supervising the maids as they changed our bed linen this morning, when there was a great clatter outside and old Tom cried, "Whoa, there!"

I ran to the window. "Father!"

"By all that noise, he is not alone," Mother said.

He wasn't. Sir Francis was below, and another man.

Mother tucked a stray wisp of hair beneath her headdress and went down. The stranger was introduced as Master Thomas Phelippes. Father had brought the gentlemen for refreshment before they continued their journeys. Mother attended to them, then came to sit in the little parlour where I was pretending to read. Were all those men really spies? Voices rumbled through the wall, and after a while we heard movement in the hall. Master Phelippes was leaving.

Mother joined Father and Sir Francis then. I stayed where I was. Well, almost. I thought I might do some sewing, and opened the closet door.

This is what I learned. Master Phelippes serves Sir Francis. He's very clever. His special gift is deciphering codes. It seems plotters and conspirators write their letters in secret codes, called ciphers, so that, should they fall into the wrong hands, they will seem meaningless. But they are not meaningless to Thomas Phelippes. He can even decipher codes in French and Latin!

I learned that Sir Francis has men in London, Paris, Rome – and who knows where else – and they all send him information. Valuable information about England's friends and enemies.

I learned that my father knows many of these men.

I also learned that Sir Francis speaks freely in front of my mother. Our family is trusted by the highest in the land.

2nd August 1585

Richard is spending a few weeks with us. The city is hot, and everyone who can has gone away to seek fresher air. He has brought work with him, and says he must make copies of many documents.

"For Sir Francis?" I asked.

He hesitated. "Some are for Sir Francis, yes."

Lord, this is a whole family of spies.

18th August 1585

Uncle William is to accompany the Lieutenant of the Tower who will be away for SIX WEEKS, and Edmund is not going with him! We may see each other every afternoon! Father is going away again tomorrow, and I know Mother and Aunt Frances will let us enjoy ourselves and not bother about Latin and French. Oh joy! But we must do something about Kathryn. She listens to everything we say, so she always knows what we're planning.

Later

I've had a marvellous idea! This afternoon I showed Edmund a loose brick in our garden wall. We can leave notes for each other tucked beneath it. If I slip one in from the inside, Edmund can reach it from the outside. As long as Kathryn doesn't see him take it, she'll never know what we are doing, or where we are going.

23rd August 1585

Early this morning I left a note for Edmund saying that after midday dinner I would walk Pawpaw in the open fields on Little Tower Hill. I hoped he would be sent on some errand, and would have a chance to find my note.

After dinner, we rested for a while. Beeba curled up while I told her a story about a wicked queen called Kathryn, with a nose as long as Beeba's leg, which she poked into everything, and one ear as big as a plate, which grew hot and red from pressing against walls while she listened to private conversations. When Lucy came to take Beeba from me, I fetched Pawpaw and off we went.

Edmund was already there! We had a lovely hour without a sign of Kathryn. The only bad thing was when Pawpaw ran across a linen sheet spread on the grass to dry. The washerwoman chased him with a stick. Luckily, she didn't catch him. He would surely have bitten her.

Edmund says he'll find some way to look under the brick every morning.

1st September 1585

Edmund and I have managed to trick Kathryn nearly every day. Today we went across London Bridge. Edmund wanted to look at the heads on spikes above the south gate, to see who he recognized from the Tower. Once we got to the other side of the bridge, we noticed crowds heading for the bear-baiting. Edmund grinned. "Shall we?"

"Swear never to tell my mother?"

He swore, and paid twopence each for us to go to the arena.

It absolutely stank. The press of the crowd, and the bits of flesh and fur scattered around the arena made me queasy, but then the fight began. I hated seeing great mastiffs tearing at the poor chained bear, and after a minute or two I turned and forced my way through the crowd, away from the stink and the blood.

Edmund came after me. He was angry. "Why did you leave?"

"It makes me feel ill."

"But there's more to see," he complained.

I didn't care. I told him he was cruel to make me watch something so horrible. I felt sick all the way home. Edmund didn't speak to me, but on the way across the bridge, he stopped at a shop and bought me a little cake of marchpane to eat.

"It'll help take the smell out of your nose," he grunted, and walked ahead.

I broke off two tiny pieces of marchpane and stuffed them inside my nostrils. When he turned round to see where I was, I said, "It works," and he burst out laughing. So that's all right. I don't like quarrelling with Edmund.

6th September 1585

Sir Francis came today bringing Mother's birthday gift. They talked together in the shade of our mulberry tree. I sat nearby, on a low wall behind the rosemary bush, with sleepy, hot Beeba on my lap. George was stuffing blackberries.

They talked first of Sir Francis's family, then he asked after the health of all of us children. He didn't ask after Father. That tells me Sir Francis knows how he is already.

My ears pricked up when Mother asked, "What news of the Scottish lady?"

Sir Francis raised his eyes to heaven. "She has bleated all summer about moving from Tutbury."

"She dislikes the house, then?" said Mother.

Sir Francis grunted. "She has few rooms, 'tis true, and Sir Amyas insists the whole place has an unhealthy air. Mind you, he would say that – he wants to move as much as she does." He stretched his legs. "I suppose she'll get her way in the end. Tilly, my dear, she is a thorn in my side. While she lives, I cannot rest. Devil woman."

He hates Mary Stuart.

"I must be constantly vigilant," Sir Francis continued. "The threat to our own lady is at the forefront of my mind."

He means the Queen.

"Much is in the air, Tilly," he said. "I must bring this business to a head."

He carried on, talking in riddles, never mentioning anyone by name. I suppose he's afraid of being overheard. He probably thinks there are spies in the very bushes. In the rosemary bush, perhaps! Kitty the Spy! Ha!

But if *he* is worried, then so am I.

8th September 1585

Edmund and I have such good times! He's fun again, just as he used to be. We are allowed to spend whole days together sometimes, and I fall into bed exhausted each night. We have rowed on the river. Well, Edmund rowed – I stared straight ahead like the Queen – and we have been hawking, which I liked. Now the sun's up and this morning we are to attend a wrestling contest, which I have never done before. And Kathryn has no idea!

How sad it will be when Uncle William returns, and Edmund goes back to his work. I preferred it before he became an apprentice.

26th September 1585

I will never sleep tonight. Edmund left a note today, saying, "Theatre. Tomorrow afternoon. Meet me at my house. No one will be there, just Dolly."

I wrote on the bottom, "I'll bring Pawpaw and leave him with Dolly. Mother will think I'm at your house."

This is a very deceitful thing I'm planning. But if Mother does not know about it, I have not disobeyed her. That's what I think.

27th September 1585

The theatre was over a mile away at Shoreditch, but I'd have walked ten miles to see it! It was hot, and the press of people where we stood to watch the play was frightening at times, but everyone was good-natured. Edmund bought me a cone of nuts to nibble, but once the play started I forgot about them.

The time flew. Next thing I knew I was clutching Edmund's shirt sleeve as I followed him out of the theatre, my head spinning. How clever is the man who wrote that play! Oh, to tell such tales. To tell a story that would make people laugh one minute and cry the next, as this did me.

Suddenly, Edmund shoved me hard. "Go back," he whispered.

"What is it?"

"My sister," he hissed. "Quick, before she—"

"I see you!" Kathryn shrieked. "Edmund Middleton, what do you think you're doing?" She marched towards us. "And you, Catherine Lumsden! Do you think to call yourself a *lady*?"

At that moment, I felt more ladylike than she was, standing in the middle of the crowd, bellowing.

"Who gave you permission to visit a – a *theatre*?" she stormed.

"Kathryn," said Edmund quietly. "You are not my father. You should not be speaking to—"

"Just wait until our mother hears about this," Kathryn snapped. "And yours, too, Kitty."

My stomach lurched. Mother was going to be very, very angry. Edmund would probably get away with it. Aunt Frances is soft.

Kathryn stalked behind us as we walked home. I tried to think of an excuse, to avoid trouble, but I couldn't.

There was something that puzzled me.

"Edmund," I whispered. "How did she know where we were?"

Later

I am in such trouble. Mother says I deserve a whipping, and I do not know yet whether she has decided not to whip me, or if she will make me wait until Father comes home. If she waits, I shall be so, so good, then maybe she will forget or, at least, forgive me.

So here I am. In my bedchamber. On my own. And these smudges on the paper are from my tears, which will not stop falling.

It's my own fault, and I know I was wrong. But can enjoying a play be so bad?

28th September 1585

Mother summoned me to the little parlour this morning. I stood before her, hands clasped, eyes lowered. She scolded me for ages. How could I go to a public place of entertainment without permission? (Thank heaven she doesn't know about the bear-baiting.) Suppose something had happened to me? She might never have seen me again. My brothers and sister would be devastated. How could she explain my injury or disappearance to Father? Worst of all, how could I have considered for one moment going into the groundlings area with the low people when there are seats for people like us?

Of course, she didn't want answers to any of these questions, and I wasn't rude or stupid enough to offer one. I am to be confined to my bedchamber for two weeks. No one may visit me apart from Mother and Sal. I must dwell upon my actions and ask God to hel—

10th October 1585

Mother entered my bedchamber as I was writing those last words and demanded my diary. I quickly knotted the riband round it before handing it over. She took my quill, my ink and left only my prayer book. I have been so bored these two weeks that I have nearly gone crazy in the head. But I've had time to think. I know how Kathryn was able to find us – she's discovered where we hide our notes. Well, I can still fool her, but I must see Richard first.

16th October 1585

I've waited almost a week to see Richard, but today he came. First he spoke with Mother in low tones. I thought something was wrong, but when she turned she was smiling.

After dinner, I got Richard alone, and asked him how to write in code. He wanted to know why, but when I confessed that it was to fool Kathryn, he fetched writing materials and sat beside me.

"You need a cipher," he said. "Here's a simple one."

Indeed it is simple. First you write the alphabet. Then you write the alphabet again beneath it, but with the letters jumbled up. Here is my cipher:

a b c d e f g h i j k l m n o p q r s t u v w x y z
p f t h a z n q c o x g y s l u w m e k v i b j r d

If I wish to write "Kitty" in code, I find the "k" in the top row and see that the letter beneath is "x". The letter beneath "i" is "c", and so on. So "Kitty" becomes "Xckkr" and "Edmund" is "Ahyvsh". Easy!

Now it won't matter if we drop our notes right in front of Kathryn's long nose! I shall compose my first one right now.

19th October 1585

I put a note under the brick two days ago. It has gone, but Edmund hasn't replied. This afternoon I shall find an excuse to visit Aunt Frances, and try to see him. Mother is still being difficult about letting me out.

Later

I may go to Aunt Frances this afternoon if I take Beeba and some of the last roses! And I am to remember to bring Beeba back. Very funny.

Much later

KITTY LUMSDEN IS THE MOST STUPID GIRL IN THE WHOLE WORLD! I have scarcely stopped laughing since I saw Edmund. Poor Beeba keeps squeezing my cheeks, trying to put my face back to normal.

No wonder Edmund didn't reply to my note. He could not read it! I didn't think to give him a copy of my cipher! But now I have, and I hope for a note tomorrow to Xckkr from Ahyvsh.

14th November 1585

I heard today (I wasn't eavesdropping – I was just close behind Mother, Joseph and Richard as we walked to Barkyng Church) that Mary Stuart has got her way. She has complained so much about Tutbury, that she will shortly be moved.

If Tutbury is that bad, I am glad for her. The weather is wet and grey at the moment. Even I don't go out much but, unlike her, I am at least able to if I wish (and if Mother permits).

27th November 1585

Sir Anthony Babington called today! I don't know how long he's been back in England. If it is a long time, then it is shameful that he has not called on Joseph before. My sweet brother is delighted to see him.

As they sat with their feet almost in the fire, Joseph said, "You remember the Scottish queen, Anthony, whom you once knew? She is to be moved again."

Sir Anthony looked up. "Indeed? To where?"

"To Chartley," said Joseph. "My brother said Sir Francis gave the order some days ago."

"I know Chartley," said Sir Anthony. "It's a good-sized house, so there will be more room for Her Majesty's servants. She has secretaries, a physician, grooms, cooks, laundresses and ladies – any number to be housed." He sighed. "But its chief attraction to Sir Francis will be the moat. It would be a difficult house to escape from." He stared into the fire.

I wonder why he thought of escape. Is he another who sees spies and enemies round every corner?

19th December 1585

Father is back and, at last, the whole family is together again! Joseph is home for the Christmas holidays and Richard has been allowed to leave court for three weeks. At first I thought, how lucky, because it coincides with Father's homecoming. But now I believe it is *because* Father is home. That leads me to believe that Father is highly regarded at court, though he is hardly ever there.

The Walsinghams will dine with us next week, because there is much for Sir Francis and Father to discuss. It sounds a dreary occasion.

23rd December 1585

The Walsinghams came. After dinner, while Father and Sir Francis talked alone, Lady Ursula Walsingham, Mother, Joseph, Richard and I sat cosily in the little parlour.

Lady Ursula asked Richard, "Why do you not sit with the men?" Then she answered herself – a habit she has. "But my husband will no doubt speak with you when you return to court." A while ago, that remark would have surprised me, but not any more.

Of course, I couldn't hear anything that was said in the next room. I sewed as Mother and Lady Ursula chatted and, although I went to the closet as often as I could, I heard only odd words.

Later, though, when the guests had left, Mother went to sit with Father, and Richard and Joseph went to the Middletons' house. They didn't particularly want to see Uncle William, but if they visit there, they may use the Tower tavern.

Since everybody else moved, so did I – into the closet. And I heard some interesting news. A man called Gilbert Gifford landed in England, from France, on the 10th of this month. Sir Francis knew that Gifford had been mixing with Mary Stuart's supporters in Paris, and he believes Gifford came here to do some "intriguing" – to plot to free Mary.

But Sir Francis is too clever for him. Hardly had Gifford set foot on English soil, when he was arrested. To get out of trouble, he immediately wrote an interesting letter to Sir Francis. As near as I can remember, it said something like, "I have heard of the work you do and I want to serve you. I have no scruples, and have no fear of danger. Whatever you order me to do, I will do." Something like that.

He was taken to Sir Francis, who plans to make good use of him. How exciting! A real spy, working for one side, then for the other. Gifford has two faces.

I shall not tell Edmund this news. I will be Kitty the Silent. My father is involved and, for all I know, Richard, too. If Edmund spreads the news, they could get into serious trouble, and it would probably spoil Sir Francis's plots and plans.

3rd January 1586

We are all invited to Sir Francis Walsingham's home, Barn Elms, for Twelfth Night, and he will send his barge for us! Aunt Frances is so jealous, but Kathryn just sniffed and said she doesn't care for merrymaking.

7th January 1586

The party was wonderful, and so grand! Mother wore a new moss-green velvet gown, with her emeralds. I wore deep rose satin, and received many compliments. I danced, ate and drank enough to make me feel sick this morning.

I also gleaned news of Mary Stuart. She and her retinue were moved to Chartley on Christmas Eve. It must have been a cold journey, and has done her no good, for she's been ill ever since.

Master Phelippes is also at Chartley. This is not common gossip, but something I overheard while standing near the library door. Why on earth has he gone there? He is certainly no friend of Mary Stuart. It must be something to do with his cipher work.

On the way home, Father told me that Queen Elizabeth has visited Barn Elms more than once. I shall tell Edmund that I have been in the same room as the Queen. I won't say that it was not at the same time.

11th January 1586

I left a note in cipher saying, "Edmund, I will be walking by Minories Cross this afternoon. If you have to go to the city, find me and keep me company a while. Kitty."

It was cold by the Cross, but I was warmly wrapped. I wandered in circles, keeping Pawpaw away from the cows that grazed nearby. I was about to give up and go home, when Edmund appeared. He carried a package, which meant he'd probably been to the apothecary for something gruesome, like dead mice, for one of his concoctions.

"Where have you been?" I asked. "Shall we have a race round the Tower? We haven't done that for ages. It will warm us."

He groaned, and at first I thought he didn't want to race me, but then I saw what caused his dismay.

"Kathryn!" I said sharply. "Where did you come from?"

She smiled her pinched smile. "I just chanced by. Shall we walk together, Kitty? Edmund, our father awaits you."

If Edmund didn't tell her we were meeting, how did she know where to find us?

14th January 1586

I was letting Pawpaw chase gulls along the river bank today, when I saw Sir Francis's barge approaching. He was standing, urging the oarsmen to go faster, faster! As the boat pulled alongside, he leapt to the bank and hurried up the hill towards our house.

I followed, and found Sir Francis clasping Father's shoulders, saying, "It's all set up, Nick. The lady will have letters from her friends within a few days. Is it not marvellous?"

"The lady" is Mary Stuart, but I just don't understand. She was banned from having letters for a whole year, and now Sir Francis is excited because she's going to get some. What's going on?

28th January 1586

Richard and Father took me riding today. I have a new pair of gloves, I was wrapped in a warm cloak, the sun shone and there was no wind. We rode north through Aldgate, by Spitalfields, and into open country. The men kept having stupid little races, but my pony just walked.

Before long, we stopped by a stream, sat on a length of blanket and ate the cold beef and apple tart we'd brought. We drank ale, and then, when Richard and Father began talking about hunting, I snuggled between them for a nap.

I must have slept, because I was suddenly aware that they were talking about Phelippes. I kept my eyes closed. This is what I remember, but I may not have the conversation exactly right.

Father said, "Phelippes is clever. He's set it all up. Letters will go in to the lady, and letters will come out. But each will be read by Phelippes, copied, and sent to Sir Francis. The original letters will go on to whoever they were addressed to."

"Surely the lady will discover that the letters are being intercepted," said Richard.

The lady – Mary Stuart again!

"Do not underestimate your master," Father replied. "Gilbert Gifford is established as a link between the French embassy and Mary Stuart. Sir Francis ordered Phelippes to devise a secret way, using Gifford, for the lady to get letters in and out of Chartley."

It seems that a brewer from Burton-on-Trent, a few miles away, regularly delivers beer to Mary Stuart. Phelippes got Gilbert Gifford, the double spy, to tell the brewer that the Queen of Scots would pay him well to smuggle out letters in his beer barrels. Then Phelippes himself went to the brewer and asked him to pass any letters that came his way to Sir Amyas Paulet. And he would be paid for this.

The brewer asked what would happen to the letters, because he was being paid to deliver them, but he was told not to worry. Sir Amyas would only keep them for a short while, then they would be returned to him. In reality, Sir Amyas would first pass them to Phelippes, to be deciphered.

So the brewer's getting paid twice for the same job. How could he resist it? And Sir Francis Walsingham gets to know every word that passes to or from Mary Stuart.

Someone stroked my cheek and Father said, "Time to go, Kitty." I made a performance of waking. I think I fooled them.

6th February 1586

After church at St Peter's, I met Edmund at the door. Everyone stood talking, so we went to sit on the steps of the Beauchamp Tower. I looked up at the window, imagining the prisoners there. Of course, those are the more important ones; others are in the dank little towers set in the curtain wall or, worse, beneath the White Tower.

"Edmund," I asked, "if you wanted to hide a letter in a beer barrel, how would you do it so it wouldn't get wet?"

He snorted. "You and your silly daydreams! I suppose it's a magic letter, from a fairy."

"Seriously," I said. "If you give the right answer, I'll tell you what it's about."

He clapped his hands at a raven that ventured too close. "Is there beer in the barrel?"

"Yes."

"Then it can't go right inside. So," Edmund said, slowly, "what you could do is make a hollow bung, and hide the letter inside."

"What's a bung?"

"I'll show you." Edmund sped off towards the Tower tavern. Outside were four large barrels. In each was a hole for pouring beer, and in each hole was a large lump of cork.

"That's a bung," said Edmund. "Now you have the answer. Tell me what it's all about."

I'm too clever for him. "I said I'd tell you if you gave me the right answer," I said. "That was the wrong one."

He pinched me! I screamed and ran for the gate, but as I passed Edmund's house, Kathryn barred my way.

"Catherine Lumsden!" she snapped. "You behave like a common street urchin! You just get worse!"

Oh, she drives me insane!

11th February 1586

This evening, Joseph came home and hurried straight to his bedchamber. I went to see if he was all right. It isn't like him to be gloomy, especially now Sir Anthony is back.

"Is something wrong?" I asked.

"Nothing to bother your pretty head with," he said.

If he only knew – my pretty head is bothered with a lot more than a brother's troubles. Eventually, I persuaded him to talk.

"Last night, Kitty," he said, "I was with my friends at Babington's lodgings. After we'd dined, some fell to gambling, and others talked. Then a man called John Savage arrived. Kitty, he is Savage by name, and savage by nature."

"What do you mean?"

"Never breathe a word of this," said Joseph. "Swear, Kitty?"

"I swear," I said.

He told me that he had heard Savage vow to kill the Queen!

"Joseph," I said, "if this is the company Sir Anthony keeps, you should not be his friend."

But Joseph insisted that Sir Anthony is not close to Savage. "Although I know Savage used to be a priest," he finished.

"Then you are mad, brother," I said. "The law says it's treason to be a Catholic priest now. You could be put to death for helping one."

Joseph said. "Savage *used* to be a priest. He's not one now. And I have not helped him – I barely spoke to him. He probably talked rubbish, anyway – perhaps he is mad. Who knows? I may never see him again." He hugged me. "Kitty, you are more trustworthy than anyone I know."

Especially Sir Anthony and his Catholic friends, I thought. Lord, I hope Joseph is not getting himself into bad trouble.

18th February 1586

Joseph has not seen John Savage again. Maybe he is not close to Babington after all.

21st February 1586

Pawpaw had a thorn in his paw today and would not let even me near him. Harry kept saying, "Poor Pawpaw's paw!" and cackling with laughter.

But then Joseph brought Sir Anthony and Chidiock Tichborne home this afternoon, and they sat by the fire, drinking and singing. When I took them a fresh jug of wine, I looked at Joseph's happy face and didn't feel so worried about him.

Pawpaw lay in a corner of the room and growled when I went near. Sir Anthony heard the growl and came over. "What's wrong, pretty Kitty?" he said. I wish he wouldn't call me that. It makes my face go red.

I told him about the thorn. He reached out to Pawpaw, and there was no growl! In moments, Sir Anthony was gently examining the thorn.

"Will you fetch warm water, Kitty, and a soft cloth?"

When I returned, Sir Anthony held Pawpaw out to me and said, "You may bathe the paw – the thorn is out!" I could have hugged him.

When Richard came in, I said, "Sir Anthony has healed Pawpaw!"

"He is brave indeed," laughed Richard, and we sat together by the window for a while, watching snowflakes fall and listening to the others chatting. When Joseph went to refill their jug, Tichborne turned to Sir Anthony and murmured, "Shall we see Ballard tonight?"

Sir Anthony hushed him, and they talked of other things. But I felt Richard sit up slightly.

Later

Richard spoke quietly to Father this evening (not quietly enough for Kitty Lumsden!) and said he'd heard Ballard's name mentioned. "He's the priest from France, isn't he? The one who plots with the Spanish?" asked Richard. "He must be in England."

"He is in London, in disguise, but is being watched," said Father. "By the way, the lady has asked the ambassador in France to send all the letters he holds for her! She trusts the brewer's delivery service completely!"

I was sitting, writing, with my back to them, but Richard must have glanced at me, because Father said, "Don't worry. Kitty's absorbed in her diary or some such."

Kitty was absorbed in writing down all she heard! I have copied it into my diary, and must make my knots very secure.

28th February 1586

Father has broken his arm and his foot! It's all my fault and I have not stopped sobbing since. He only went away yesterday, and I had no idea he would be back home today. I rounded the corner by the stable and came upon him, just as he dismounted. I shrieked in delight, and the horse took fright. Father still had one foot in the stirrup, and his other foot went from beneath him. He fell heavily, and I swear I heard the arm crack.

He's now in bed asleep, after drinking some horrible potion that Uncle William brought. In the morning, I will tell him how truly sorry I am.

1st March 1586

Father swears the accident was not my fault. I've vowed to be at his side constantly, and to do anything he asks of me. Today I read the Bible to him.

2nd March 1586

I offered to read to Father again, but he does not want to wear me out. All he needed was his pillow fluffed up. I shall make pottage for him today with my own hands, if the cook will let me.

Later

My pottage is on the fire, smelling delicious. The cook gave me some bones, and I've put all the vegetables I could find into it. Father will enjoy it.

3rd March 1586

Father said my pottage was very tasty, and asked for more. Harry said he was just being polite.

4th March 1586

Father asked me to write a letter for him today, telling someone I've never heard of that he's indisposed. He managed to sign his name with his poor arm. My handwriting is neat and well-formed, he says, and he has promised more work for me.

12th March 1586

Today Father asked me to write in reply to a letter from Sir Francis Walsingham. His words seemed very mysterious (at first) and, after he'd signed it, he asked me to add, "Dictated to Catherine Lumsden by the above named". Then, when Ann had taken the letter downstairs, Father asked me to take Sir Francis's own letter and lock it in his chest in the library.

I could not resist glancing at the letter. Well,

actually, I read it but, to be fair, no one said I could not. I learned that Mary Stuart writes her letters in code, and that Master Phelippes found it extremely easy to break her cipher. He got hold of 21 letters sent to her from France and copied them. Now they are being forwarded to her in the next beer barrel. Imagine how excited she'll be to receive them.

I almost feel sorry for the lady. She happily sends letters off in a beer barrel. They are read and copied before being sent onwards. Any replies are treated in the same way, then put into the barrel and sent to Mary.

Sir Francis Walsingham knows everything she is thinking. And he also knows a great deal of what her supporters think.

2nd May 1586

Yesterday was a perfect May Day. We took a boat to the fair near Westminster. The river was busier than ever, and it was difficult to find somewhere to moor. We had quite a walk to Tothill Fields. Lucy took charge of Beeba and George, Harry stayed with Father, and I walked with Mother.

Every stall was decorated with garlands of flowers. There was much to buy, and games to play, like bowling to win a pig. A tall pink-and-green maypole stood in the middle, waiting for the dancers.

We were wandering round when, from the far side of the green, we heard great cheers! Father crouched down so George could climb on his shoulders.

"Who can you see?" Father asked.

"Gentlemen and ladies," said George.

"Is that all?" Father asked.

"Gentlemen bowing," he said. "Bowing to a lady."

Someone cried, "'Tis the Queen!" I didn't believe it, but suddenly the people in front of us parted and made way for a group of handsomely dressed ladies and gentlemen, who walked slowly towards us. And there, in the middle – I could not mistake her, for she glittered and shone in the sunshine – was Queen Elizabeth herself! She nodded and smiled to either side, but she didn't stop.

As she passed us, she caught sight of Father. "Good morrow, Sir Nicholas," she said. "Are you enjoying the celebrations?"

He bowed deeply. "I am, Your Majesty, I thank

you," he replied, and she moved on. I stared at her (with my mouth open, as Harry told me later) and completely forgot to curtsy. Mother said it didn't matter, as Her Majesty would not notice.

"She didn't notice you, either, Madam," I said.

Mother smiled. "She remembers me every year on our birthday. Come, the dancers are beginning."

Father said the Queen gave a May Ball at Whitehall in the evening. I expect she wanted some fresh air before she got ready.

On the way home I said, "The Queen is brave to walk among the people. Suppose someone wanted to kill her? Nothing would be easier."

Father nodded towards the boatmen, and whispered to me to hold my tongue. "The Queen is guarded constantly," he said. "There were expert swordsmen about her today, who would die protecting her. She is safe."

From what Edmund says, that's not true. The Tower's full of people who believe otherwise.

I think the Queen very grand. Her dress sparkled with silver thread and pearls, and her leather shoes were embroidered in gold. But she is not beautiful. In truth, she is old. I worked out that she is 52, which is a great age.

14th May 1586

I left a note (in cipher) for Edmund today, asking him to come when he was free. Just after midday, he slipped through the back gate.

"I got your message," he said. "I cannot stay long..." He saw my expression. "What is it?"

"Someone else got the message, too," I said. "Unless she followed you."

He turned and groaned. Kathryn! "She could not have followed me," he said. "I've just come from Eastcheap."

"Where's my note?" I asked.

"At home," he said. "But she could not read it. It's in code."

This happens time and again. How does she do it?

Mother called from the house, "Good day Kathryn. Come and advise me where to hang my new picture." From her nose, would be my suggestion.

Edmund couldn't stay, but I wasn't alone for long. There was a commotion as Joseph arrived with a whole group of acquaintances, including, of course, Sir Anthony. I tidied myself, and went to see if there was anything they wanted, but they'd already sent for wine. It was a moment before I realized that Kathryn was close behind me.

Joseph asked teasingly, "What have you been doing, Kitty? Writing your diary?"

"No," I said. "Talking to Edmund."

Sir Anthony smiled. "What do you write in your diary, Kitty?"

Anything of interest that anyone says, I thought. Including you. Aloud, I said, "Just things that make up my day."

"Come, tell me," he said. "What does pretty Kitty do? What will you write today?"

"Let me see," I replied. "I'll write about the new stitch I'm learning ... and how I taught a song to Beeba ... and played ball with Pawpaw ... and about Mother's new songbird..."

There, I thought! That's the sort of thing "pretty Kitty" might write. I didn't mention quarrelling with Harry, or the trouble I had persuading (or bullying) Sal to mend the new dress I tore exploring a broken-down building in the Tower yesterday.

Kathryn began to simper. "My own diary, Sir Anthony," she said, "might interest you. I have a full and interesting life."

He smiled. "I'm sure you do."

Ha! If she keeps a diary, it's probably full of things like, "I told tales about Kitty" or "My embroidery is far better than anything Kitty will ever do" (which is true). I went to sit in my favourite corner by the window. Kathryn joined me, and sat so Sir Anthony would see her profile. She has a turned-up nose that she thinks is pretty. I think it's like that of a piglet.

The men droned on. I think most of them are Sir Anthony's friends. Poor Joseph was not much in their conversation. They are too quick and witty.

After a while, Kathryn announced, "I must go home now."

The men rose.

"It is not far," she said.

I know she hoped Sir Anthony would escort her, but Joseph offered instead. I expect she was furious.

I stayed where I was, snuggled in behind a wall-hanging, cuddling Pawpaw and gazing through the window. I drifted into a dream where I was walking beside a high wall, when I heard a voice cry, "Will no one help me?" I climbed over the wall (ripping my bodice as I did so) and, when I leapt lightly down, I found a prince bound to a tree. I knew he was a prince because he had a crown on. I was struggling to free him before his evil captor appeared, when I heard someone say, "Ballard".

"We've all been visited by Ballard," murmured Robert Barnwell. "Babington, you must be our leader."

"Why are you so troubled?" asked Thomas Salisbury. "In four months it will all be over. Ballard promised. He's in touch with our country's friends abroad – and is trusted by them."

"Sh!" said Sir Anthony. "This is not the time."

They went quiet, and I guessed he was pointing at the bulge in the curtain that was me. But then Joseph came in. "Where's Kitty?" he asked. "There you are. Mother wants you in your bedchamber." That meant she wanted to scold me for the mess it's in.

I said goodbye to Joseph's so-called friends. I don't know what they were discussing, but it was something Catholic, that's for sure. They mentioned the priest, Ballard.

I'm frightened. I fear they are persuading Joseph to become a Catholic. Why else would they come here so often?

Later

I asked Joseph what he thinks of Roman Catholics. "I do not think of them at all," he said. "If you speak of my friends, I enjoy their company, and they enjoy mine. They break no laws."

18th May 1586

Kathryn did it again! Edmund left me a message in our special cipher, telling me when and where to meet. Minutes after I arrived with Pawpaw, there she was! I had to find out how she knew where we would be.

"Kathryn, you keep coming upon us by accident."

"'Tis not by accident," she said.

"It must be," I said. "No one can have such knowledge – unless she is a witch! You do not want to be tried as a witch, do you?"

That scared her. "I know *nothing* of witchcraft," she said.

"Then how do you know where we meet?" demanded Edmund.

She smirked. "I deciphered your silly code."

I did not believe her, and said so.

"Kitty, my dear," she said, as if I were three and she were 33, "your very first message was addressed to Edmund and signed 'Kitty'. That gave me nine letters without any effort. You see, the letter 'x' was substituted for 'k', and—"

How stupid we have been! Of course she might guess those words.

"—as soon as I had those, I recognized the words 'Minories', 'afternoon' and 'the', which gave me five more letters." She laughed. "That was over half the alphabet already. The rest was a simple matter."

Edmund and I had nothing to say. But as we followed her home, our eyes burned holes in her bodice.

10th June 1586

Joseph looked downcast when he brought Harry home from school this evening.

"What is it, brother?" I asked.

He would say nothing at first, but gradually I drew it from him. He is being ignored again by Sir Anthony and his friends.

"I do not understand," he said. "I'm never invited to join them these days, or dine with them. They happily accept my hospitality – indeed I sometimes feel they treat this house as a meeting place, a change from taverns and rented rooms." He put his arm round me. "The worst thing is that Babington has arranged to have a portrait painted of himself with all his friends – and I am not included."

What could I say? Poor simple, trusting Joseph.

16th June 1586

I am fearful for Joseph. Today I asked him to take me riding. We talked – my pony side-by-side with his horse – of how hard he finds his studies. He doesn't want to be a lawyer, but would like perhaps to help Father in his work.

Dear Joseph, not only does he not have the sharp mind that's needed for whatever Father does, but he also has no natural suspicion of others. He thinks everyone is good and that only circumstances make them do bad things.

Eventually I brought up the subject of Sir Anthony, the Catholics and the Queen.

"I am afraid, Joseph," I said. "Something bad is happening. I fear they are involved."

He was silent, and in that moment, a dreadful thought struck me.

"Joseph!" I cried. "Please tell me *you* are not involved. Please tell me you're not planning to harm the Queen. Please..."

He reined in his horse and stared at me with a

dreadful look on his face. "Kitty, how can you even think such a thing?"

I burst into tears. He dismounted and lifted me down. We sat on a stile and I poured out my fears. Joseph is unable to believe ill of his friends, so I said, "If they are innocent, there can be no harm in telling Father, can there?"

But Joseph made me swear not to. "You say that Sir Francis knows all that's going on?"

"Yes."

"He knows about this Ballard?"

"Yes."

"Then," said Joseph, "Sir Francis has everything well in hand. So swear you will say nothing."

"I will say nothing if you promise not to see Sir Anthony again."

"I will make no attempt to see him, Kitty. I promise."

Slowly, we rode home.

27th June 1586

Sir Francis called to see Father today, on his way home from Greenwich, and I have felt sick ever since. I was supposed to be keeping Beeba and George quiet while Mother visits the Middletons, but I told a maid to do it instead. She protested that she was supposed to be scraping old rushes off the kitchen floor, and picking herbs to mix with new ones. "They stink," she said. "Mrs Sal will kill me if I don't do it."

"I'll pick the herbs," I said. "Now go." I slipped into the little parlour and wedged a stool against the door, so no one would catch me eavesdropping.

I learned that Mary Stuart is very unwell. She is 43 now, and often sickly. What surprised me – no, what *shocked* me – was to hear Sir Anthony's name.

"Babington contacted Robert Poley who, as you know, Nick, has served me for some while," said Sir Francis. "He tends to encourage Catholics as acquaintances, so he can discover what they are up to. Babington asked Poley to arrange a licence for him and his friend Salisbury to travel abroad."

I was relieved. If Anthony Babington wants to go abroad, he cannot, I thought, be planning trouble here. But my heart fluttered when Father spoke.

"It's likely he wishes to stir up the lady's supporters abroad, and to have an escape route in case his plans go wrong."

"He shall not," said Sir Francis firmly. "I saw Babington myself today, and refused the licence. The man was nervous, and did not take my refusal well. He will be back."

"And is there news from the Continent?"

"There is. Gifford has been to Paris – on my orders – and he reports that the French will not invade unless Her Majesty is dead, and only if the rescue of Mary Stuart is absolutely certain. But the Spanish are less cautious. Gifford believes they could invade before the end of September and attempt to put the devil woman on the throne."

"And if Babington goes ahead with his plan to have John Savage kill the Queen," said Father thoughtfully, "and to ride to Mary's rescue himself..."

Sir Francis laughed. "He will not, Nick. We watch him as a hawk watches a shrew. We know his every move. And we read every scrap of correspondence that goes in and out of Chartley."

I crept back upstairs. They know his every move. That means they know he is friendly – was friendly – with Joseph. My one thought was to tell my brother. But then he might warn Sir Anthony that he is in danger. Oh, what to do?

1st July 1586

We were breaking our fast this morning, when Mother said to Joseph, "We haven't seen Sir Anthony lately. Why not invite him to dine? We might ask the Middletons. Kathryn would be delighted!"

I am confused. Father talks to my mother. She must know that Sir Anthony is under suspicion. Why does she want Joseph to stay close to him?

4th July 1585

I swear my legs turned to jelly today when Sir Anthony was shown in. It was pouring outside, great sheets of rain, and the last thing we expected was a visitor.

I wanted to stay with Joseph while they talked, but Mother said, "Let them alone," and went into the little parlour to work on the wall hanging. I fidgeted until she told me to make myself useful and tidy her work basket.

When Sir Anthony left, I cornered Joseph as he closed the front door. "What was it? What did he want?"

Joseph shrugged. "He was miserable, and wanted to see a friendly face. He's been again to ask Sir Francis about a travel licence."

"Did he get it?"

Joseph shook his head. "No, and he is distraught. When I asked what the trouble was, he said, 'I wish I could tell you, Joseph, but I cannot.'"

I was just thinking, Thank goodness, when there was a quiet but urgent knocking on the front door. Joseph opened it, and there stood Sir Anthony, dripping wet.

He stumbled inside and clutched Joseph's arms. I slipped back into the shadows.

"Joseph, you know Sir Francis," Sir Anthony gabbled desperately. "Cannot you put in a plea for me? I swear, if he gives me a licence and allows me to go free, I will inform him of a plot to kill the Queen!"

Joseph was confused. "I – I have no influence..."

"Your brother, then," Sir Anthony insisted. "Or your father?"

"They are not here."

Sir Anthony's head drooped. Slowly, he straightened and held his head high. "One way or another, this must be resolved. Joseph, I am sorry that you see fit to let me down."

He turned and walked out into the grey, driving rain.

Later

Father has just returned. He told Mother that he arrived home to see old Tom stabling Babington's horse. Father had expected that he would start begging people to intercede for him with Walsingham, so he went to the Middletons' until Babington left. Oh, and Ballard will be arrested tomorrow. I heard all this because I was putting away the wall hanging. Slowly.

When I went upstairs, Joseph called me into his chamber. "I feel bad, Kitty," he said. "I have let Anthony down."

"That is what *he* says," I told my poor brother. "It is not the truth."

Joseph was unconvinced, I could see.

5th July 1586

Father received a letter from Sir Francis this morning. When he'd read it, he spoke briefly with Mother, then called Joseph and me into the library.

"What I say must remain within these walls," he said. "Joseph, you will leave your studies for a while. I will tell you when you may return to them. Kitty, speak to no one of this – not to Edmund, or your Aunt Frances, no one. Do you both understand?"

"Yes, Father," we said.

It was about Anthony Babington. We are to have nothing more to do with him. Joseph must stay out of his company.

"Please tell me why," Joseph said.

Father hesitated, but Mother said, "It is best, Nicholas. Joseph and Kitty must understand how serious this is."

Father informed us that Babington is plotting to rescue Mary Stuart and make her Queen of England.

Joseph went white. "I know nothing of this, I swear..."

"Of course you do not," Mother said gently. "I'm sorry that we have continued to allow Babington to come here, but it has been necessary for certain people to find out all they can."

"And Babington is not careful when or where he speaks," said Father. "Bad for him, but helpful for those who seek to protect our queen."

"May I ask something, Father?" I said.

He nodded.

"Why does no one arrest Babington, so that he cannot carry out his plan?"

Father took a deep breath. "Because, Kitty, Sir Francis has a bigger plan, and Babington is part of it.

Rest assured, steps are being taken to prevent anything bad happening. Your family is safe, and your queen is safe. Just have nothing to do with Babington." He turned to Joseph. "I promise I will tell you of any news."

Good. Then Joseph can tell me.

6th July 1586

Joseph is almost light-hearted at the thought of no more studies for a while. It's too hard for him. There are so many books, and he is a slow reader.

I have wondered all night about the "bigger plan" Father mentioned.

13th July 1586

Father has a message from Sir Francis's home, Barn Elms. Babington has been there, trying again to get a travel licence. I truly do not understand. He was there, face to face with the man who must keep Queen Elizabeth safe. Why was he not arrested? Sir Francis's bigger plan, I suppose.

16th July 1586

Richard knows much of what goes on. He talks quite openly to Joseph, which is useful, because I ask Joseph to tell me. He says I don't ask him, I bully him, but who cares? After all, it was me who realized Babington is a Catholic, me who felt there was something wrong about him, me who warned Joseph.

The interesting thing is that Babington is closer to Mary Stuart then even I dreamed. Earlier this month he wrote to her. Imagine! That's like Joseph writing a letter to Queen Elizabeth! But it's the contents of his letter that are frightening. He told Mary all about the plot to free her and – this was the terrible thing – he talked of the preparations being made abroad to invade England. He wrote of the plans he was making to "ensure the dispatch of the usurping competitor" I asked Joseph who Babington meant by "competitor". It is Queen Elizabeth, and by "dispatch", he means murder.

Babington and his friends intend to kill the Queen.

Later

I have been wondering how Mary Stuart will reply to Babington's letter. If I were in her shoes, I would tell him not to be stupid – it's too dangerous. Surely she remembers the Bond of Association.

Joseph said, "Elizabeth is her cousin, for goodness' sake. No one would execute their own cousin!"

Dear Joseph. I am quite sure that if it was Mary's life or Elizabeth's life, Mary's neck would feel the axe.

31st July 1586

Master Phelippes dined here today. The instant he arrived, he grasped Father's hands and said, "We have her, Nick!"

I was bursting to know what he was talking about, but dared not ask. I stayed silent, as usual, until I was spoken to, which wasn't often.

At dinner, Master Phelippes drank much wine and said to Mother, "I have been under pressure lately, Madam. I am unable to express how good it is to relax and spend time with you and your husband. Richard, too – we are usually working when we meet, are we not?"

"Indeed, sir," said Richard.

I was still wondering, what did he mean when he said, "We have her"? Who is "her"?

It seems to me there might be three plots now: one to free Mary Stuart and make her queen, a second to kill Elizabeth, and then another. I'm not sure what the third plot is, but there is something, and I will find out.

After dinner, Mother went to play with the little ones while Lucy ate. Joseph and I moved into the small parlour. I sat near the closet with some mending. Joseph read aloud to me, which was annoying, for while he droned haltingly on, I couldn't hear even a mumble from the next room.

Eventually, I could stand it no more. "Joseph?" I beckoned, and opened the closet.

He looked bemused for a moment, then his eyes widened.

Just then, the door opened and Mother looked in.

"I'm showing Joseph what wonderful colours we have," I babbled, waving a handful of silks.

"Master Phelippes is leaving," she said. "Come and say your farewells."

We hurried out. As soon as Phelippes had left, Mother joined Father. Joseph and I rushed into the little parlour and flung open the closet door.

"...her cipher was easy to break," Father was saying. "I almost feel sorry for the woman – she doesn't stand a chance against Sir Francis. The reply to Babington shows quite clearly that she approves of the plot to free her."

Mother's voice said, "Then it must also show that she approves of the plot to kill Queen Elizabeth." She paused. "I feel no pity for her. It is treason indeed. Did the lady say more?"

"She insisted that Babington's conspirators must always have good horsemen standing by, to tell her when Elizabeth was dead – may God bless and protect our sovereign lady."

"Amen," said Mother.

For a moment, I heard only Joseph's breath in my ear. Then Father said slowly, "Tilly, there is more. But it must never leave this room."

"You know it will not," said Mother.

"Sir Francis made Phelippes add a postscript to the lady's letter. It was delivered to Babington at his lodgings in Heron's Rents two days ago."

Forgery!

Father continued. "The postscript asks for names of the conspirators. Once Sir Francis has those, all can be tried for treason."

I closed the closet door and turned to Joseph. His face was milk-white.

"Kitty," he whispered. "I think I must know all those conspirators. I have probably talked with them, drunk with them, dined with them. Kitty, I swear…"

My poor brother was beside himself with terror. I tried desperately to reassure him. "You are Sir Nicholas Lumsden's son," I said. "Our father is friends with important people. He and Richard are both, I am sure, trusted servants of Sir Francis – one of the highest in the land. Don't be afraid. You've done nothing wrong."

"I know that." His voice trembled. "But if anyone says I have, how can I prove otherwise? I am – was – Anthony's friend. I must have been seen with him countless times."

I soothed him but, in truth, I fear for him, too.

Later

Joseph made me promise to say nothing of his terrors to anyone. "If people know I am afraid, I will appear guilty," he said.

I vowed to say nothing. I would not harm Joseph for the world.

1st August 1586

The weather is hot and sticky, but Father prefers that I stay home. All appears calm, but I know that elsewhere two queens are in danger.

Joseph, Richard and Edmund have gone over to the south bank of the river, where the water is clearer, to swim. I so envy them. What would it be like to strip down to my chemise, and to slip into the cool water?

I should drown, of course, for I do not know how to swim.

3rd August 1586

Richard burst in while Father was eating. "Gilbert Gifford has disappeared!" he announced.

Gifford is the man who switched sides when he was arrested – a man no one should trust.

Father immediately left for court. Richard is to sleep at home while he is gone, and old Tom will guard our door at night.

Later

Everyone speaks openly these days – within this house, of course. Richard said that Gifford visited the French embassy with John Savage before he vanished. (Does Sir Francis have spies *every*where?) They arranged for Gifford to pose as a servant to the embassy messenger and escape with him to France.

"He must know that Mary Stuart will soon realize he was a traitor to her, after pretending to be her ally, Richard said. "He was the one who arranged delivery of her letters—"

"—in the beer barrel," I finished for him.

Richard frowned. "You know too much, Kitty. How did you know about that?"

I shrugged and changed the subject. "What happened to John Savage?"

"He's still here."

That worries me. I hope Sir Francis's men watch Savage closely. He sounds as if he is the real danger. After all, he vowed to kill the Queen with his own hands.

Joseph asked, his voice shaky, if Richard thought Babington would flee, too.

Richard laughed. "He might try, but warrants for his and Ballard the priest's arrests are already prepared. Thanks to the exchange of letters between Mary Stuart and Babington, Sir Francis has all the evidence he needs to try the lady for treason. He only waits for Babington to reply to her request for the names of those involved. Then he will know all the conspirators, and can make his move."

Joseph said not a word.

And I? I now know that I'm right. There are three plots. The third is Sir Francis Walsingham's plot to bring Mary Stuart to her doom.

4th August 1586

I was awakened by sharp tugs on my earlobe. I shot up and opened my mouth to scream, but a hot hand was clapped over it.

"Hush!" hissed a voice. "It's me."

"Joseph? What o'clock is it?"

"Late. Early. I don't know," he muttered. "Kitty, I must do something tomorrow, and you must make sure I'm not discovered."

I had a bad feeling. "What?"

"I have to see Anthony, just once more."

"Joseph! It's more than your life is worth to warn him..."

"Kitty, I swear I will give no hint of what I know. But I have thought long about what he said, and I must convince him that I have not let him down. I have to do this."

"You *don't*!" I said. "Joseph, he is *bad*!"

He sighed. "He's only bad because he is on the other side. If he was plotting to kill someone to save Queen Elizabeth, we'd say he is good, and we would praise him, and he would be given great rewards. Don't you see, Kitty? He believes he is right, just as Father and Richard and Sir Francis believe they are right. He believes God is on his side, as we believe He is on ours."

What could I say? "You are my brother. I cannot refuse you."

As I struggled to go back to sleep, I murmured, "But I will go with you, Joseph, and watch over you."

Afternoon

Mother took the children to spend the day with the Middletons. She said Edmund would be working, so I could choose whether to visit Kathryn, or stay with Richard and Joseph.

"Let me see," I said, pretending to decide.

Mother laughed. "Be good," she said, and they were gone. A few minutes later, Richard said he needed to go out, and asked if we were happy to stay by ourselves.

Of course I was, but Joseph was annoyed. "What shall I do?" he said. "I must go, but I hate to leave you alone."

"You shall not leave me," I said. "I'm coming with you."

I soon wished I hadn't spent the next half-hour arguing with him, for my legs ached long before we reached Heron's Rents soon after midday. As we climbed the gloomy stairs, a young student Joseph knows bounced down.

"Is Sir Anthony Babington above?" asked Joseph.

The young man laughed. "I should think not. One of his friends was arrested right by that door not an hour since." He pointed to where we'd just come in. "Babington was upstairs, and seems to have taken fright. He shouted to another friend, 'To Paul's Walk!' and something about feeling savage."

We went out into the bright sunlight. "Let's go home," I said.

But Joseph was more determined than I've ever seen him. "No, Kitty. It's not far. We can find him."

My poor feet.

Soon St Paul's Church loomed before us. We went through the great doors and into Paul's Walk. I wondered how we would find Babington in that press. Everyone in London seemed to be there. People shouting that they needed servants. People shouting, "Servant for hire". Cutpurses looking for victims.

"There he is!" said Joseph suddenly.

Babington was huddled with a group of men beside a great pillar halfway down an aisle.

"Wait here, Kitty," said Joseph. "I will say what I have to say and then we can go home and forget we ever knew the man."

Babington was speaking so urgently that I became afraid. One of the men clenched his fist, and made downward stabbing movements.

Stabbing! I sensed instantly that this man was a killer. And then I remembered the student's words, "feeling savage".

Not "feeling savage". *Meeting* Savage.

"Joseph!" I ran after him and grabbed his arm. "Don't! They're the plotters!"

Joseph pulled away. "I just need one minute with Anthony."

"But Richard said they're being watched. Constantly! Don't you see? If you approach that group now, it will be taken for sure that you are a conspirator!"

He turned pale, but didn't move.

"Joseph! They may even have seen you making towards Babington. Come away. Now!"

Thank heaven, he did. Now we are home, and I

forgot to hide my worn shoes, and Mother keeps on about the money they cost, and how thoughtless I am, and what was I *doing* with them – polishing bricks?

Evening

Father came home exhausted. He still has his riding boots on, which he never wears indoors, because they make too much noise.

"Ballard was arrested this morning," he told Mother, making no attempt to keep it from the rest of us. "He will no longer prance around London in his thin disguise."

"Where did they arrest him?" Mother asked.

"Heron's Rents." Father chuckled. "Babington was upstairs when it happened. Sir Francis feared he might take fright and flee before we're ready to take him, so he sent a charming note to Babington saying the arrest was nothing to do with him, but in case of trouble he, Babington, would be advised to keep company with the man who delivered the letter. That man is one of Sir Francis's agents." Father stretched and Mother knelt to remove the boots. "Sir Francis promised to let me know first thing tomorrow how Babington reacts. Lord, what's that smell?"

"I cannot imagine," said Mother.

I could. It was his feet.

5th August 1586

I slept late. Anne got a stinging ear because she tried too hard to wake me. By the time I was dressed, Father had heard news of Babington. He had dined with the agent who brought the note from Sir Francis, and seemed quite at ease. But then a message arrived for the agent.

While the man read it, Babington excused himself. The agent waited, certain Babington had only gone to relieve himself. After all, he had left his sword and cape behind, so he must soon return.

Time passed, and it became clear that Babington had fled. Had he read the message upside down? Who knows? He has not been seen since.

I gradually became aware that Joseph had left the room. I went upstairs and found him frantically stuffing clothing into a bag.

"What are you doing?" I cried.

"He might come here, Kitty. He'll be desperate. I owe him this – just some clothes and money to help him get away." His expression was pleading. "The Queen is surely safe now – Babington can do no harm. It cannot hurt if he escapes."

"Dear Joseph. He won't come. You just *want* him to so you can make amends. But there's nothing to make amends for. He *won't* come." I took the bag. "If it makes you feel better, we'll leave this ready, in case he does."

He had better not!

Later

As we dined this noon, Father suddenly gave a great shout of laughter. "Do you know what that fool Babington did? He had a portrait painted of himself and his fellow conspirators. That very portrait is now being shown around as an aid to catching them! Ha!"

I heard a gurgle, and turned to see that Joseph had vomited on the floor.

Mother leapt up, but I was there first. "I'll see to him," I said.

Joseph clutched me as we went upstairs. I shouted for Sal to clean up, and took him to his chamber. He started to speak.

"Ssh," I said. "I know. You think you could so easily have been in that portrait." And I stroked my brother's forehead until he fell asleep.

9th August 1586

Each day has been the same and we have simply done our best to pass the time. But today, Father hurried in, downed a flagon of beer and said, "Kitty, bring your brother to the library."

Joseph begged me to go with him, so I did.

Father behaved as if I wasn't there. "Joseph, can you imagine Her Majesty's feelings at this moment?"

"N-no, sir."

"She is distraught," said Father. "In fact, she's in terror for her life. Babington, Savage and the rest are still at liberty and she fears they might strike at any moment. No one can put her mind at rest. Joseph, we have the names of six conspirators, but there are more. I believe you might know who they are."

Joseph backed away. "Sir, I know nothing of the conspiracy, I swear I do not—"

Father held up a hand. "I do not say you do. I say you *might* know some names. Think, son. Who were Babington's closest allies?"

Gradually Joseph gathered his wits and gave Father the names of those he'd met with Babington. "But I cannot believe they are all involved," he said.

Father picked up the list he'd made. "Probably not, Joseph, but it's likely that several of these should not be allowed to walk our city streets. Thank you."

As we went upstairs, Joseph murmured, "Dear God, what have I done? Even Father will believe I am one of them."

"Of course he will not," I said.

14th August 1586

Edmund says they have caught a conspirator! It is Chidiock Tichborne, who sat in this very house with us. I begged to be allowed to go back to the Middletons' with Edmund, and was permitted.

Geoffrey was on guard duty. "Come to see the plotter?" he asked.

"He is here?"

"Where better for a traitor?" said Geoffrey.

"Which tower is he in?"

"Now I can't tell you that." Geoffrey wagged a finger.

"There's no need," said Edmund. "I know he is in the Martin Tower."

"Martin, pah!" said Geoffrey. "That's nowhere near as secure as the Beauchamp."

We smiled, said goodbye and headed straight for the green in front of the Beauchamp Tower. We were soon shooed away, but I believe I caught a glimpse of Tichborne at the window high above. He must be in despair. Few leave the Beauchamp Tower to freedom.

At Edmund's house, Kathryn was spiteful about the

state of my hair which, it's true, I have not bothered much with today. But I got my own back. "It seems you were wrong about Sir Anthony Babington being a true gentleman," I said.

"You met him, Kathryn?" Aunt Frances was appalled.

"I may have done," she said, sticking her nose in the air. "I do not remember."

"You do!" said Edmund. "You blushed every time he looked at you."

Kathryn stalked from the room, pinching Edmund's arm as she passed. He winced, but grinned. Good old Edmund!

15th August 1586

Last evening, Father returned late, and then there was a commotion in the middle of the night. I wrapped myself in my coverlet and hurried to the landing.

Father was pulling on his boots, Mother was trying to make him take a drink, and the front doorway was full of men.

I ran down. "Father!" But he'd gone before I reached the bottom stair. "Where are they taking him?" I cried.

Mother put her arms around me. "Hush, Kitty, they are not *taking* him! Sir Francis Walsingham needs him."

I cannot sleep. Now I feel ill. Perhaps I am hungry.

Dawn

It is almost light. I feel better now that I have had a cold roast partridge.

Later

I am bored being confined to the house. Babington will never let himself be seen around here, surely? The bells of St Peter's are ringing. I wonder why... Now there are more bells... And more! What's happened? The bells sound joyous, so it cannot be anything bad like an invasion.

Very late

They are caught! All the conspirators have been brought to the city – I suppose to the Tower. Everyone in London is going wild! Even Mother came out with us. We met all the Middletons except Uncle William, who is needed in the Tower, and made our way through the thronged streets.

Such rejoicing! People have lit bonfires and are singing and dancing. Everyone shouts, "God save the Queen!" I cannot help thinking that God has a lot of help from Her Majesty's loyal subjects, like Sir Francis and my father.

We wandered like a band of apprentices on their holiday. Joseph tried, I could see, to enjoy the celebration, but he was uneasy. Mother wouldn't let us buy any food from street sellers, but Aunt Frances has no such scruples, and the morsels she slipped us kept our hunger at bay. Kathryn was disgusted, but Aunt Frances threatened to throttle her if she said anything.

When some nearby thatch caught fire, it was

enough for Mother. "Let's return home and hold our own celebration," she said. So that is what we did.

Perhaps our lives can get back to normal now.

17th August 1586

Mother has had a letter from Father. He is at a house called Tixall, near Chartley. A few days ago, Mary Stuart was out hunting with her ladies and her doctor, with Sir Amyas Paulet close behind with guards. Sir Amyas told Father that when horsemen appeared, Mary's face lit up. She probably thought they had come to tell her Queen Elizabeth was dead. Instead they had come to order her to be confined, and to go through all her possessions. She rode on, with her doctor, to Tixall, and will remain there until she is permitted to return to Chartley.

She is in great trouble, I think.

26th August 1586

Mary Stuart has returned to Chartley, and Father is home. He said she was livid when she discovered that the chest where she keeps her papers was empty, and her money all gone, but she showed no fear. Father said she became dignified and calm, even when told she will be tried for treason in a few weeks.

I'm sure I would not be dignified and calm. I would be screaming for my father and mother. But Mary Stuart has no one.

7th September 1586

Mother's birthday, and Sir Francis Walsingham brought her gift. She expected it to be forgotten this year, with all the plots and danger, but not so.

Sir Francis looked ill. He has a bad leg, and was limping horribly. Old Tom saddled a horse to carry him back to his barge. He's on his way home for a rest and to prepare for the trial of Babington and the conspirators.

15th September 1586

The conspirators' trials are over. Fourteen men have been sentenced to be hanged, bowelled and quartered. Richard has been at the Tower today, and spent an hour with us. "Somebody cares for Babington," he told us.

"Who?" Mother asked.

"His wife, in Derbyshire," said Richard. "She took a letter to the Queen, begging her to spare him."

Well! While Babington was enjoying himself in London, he had a wife at home. Wait till I tell Kathryn!

19th September 1586

Edmund heard from Geoffrey that Babington, too, has written to the Queen this very day, begging for his life. He could not have expected mercy, because his warder took another letter (which he read) to a friend. In it, Babington offered a thousand pounds if the friend could arrange his freedom.

Too late. Tomorrow, the first seven conspirators will die. I hope I can go. I'll ask Mother this evening, when she's had a cup or two of wine.

Later

I am so angry. All the Middletons are to follow the prisoners to the executions, but I may not! Everybody in the world will be there.

I curtsied beautifully to Mother, and asked,

"Madam, please may I attend the executions tomorrow with my uncle?" (I knew she would not go, nor Joseph.) She refused! "Feelings are running high," she said, "now it is known in what peril the Queen has been. I would not expose you to danger. I am sure you understand."

I curtsied again. "I do, Madam."

Of course I do NOT! I came straight up to my room and have cried ever since. It is so unfair.

20th September 1586

I slipped out this morning while Mother was still in her chamber, and watched the procession leave the Tower. The crowd's mood was quiet at first, but when the gates opened and the horses clattered over the cobbles, the noise grew like the howling and baying of dogs when they scent their quarry. The prisoners were bound to hurdles, dragged behind the horses. They would have a long and painful ride.

All I glimpsed were two white faces. Neither was Babington's, but he was there, for he is to be executed today. Will he be brave and calm, or will he scream for mercy?

Later

Edmund and Kathryn came to tell us about the executions. They had never seen such crowds, but they managed to worm their way through to the front.

"I wish we had not," said Kathryn. "It was gruesome..."

Well, of course, I thought. It was an execution! But it seems it was a little more than that. Ballard went first, and Edmund said he hung for hardly any time before he was cut down. His bowels were hacked out before his very eyes, while he was still conscious.

"Enough, Edmund," said Kathryn. "Spare Aunt Tilly any more details."

For once I was glad she's so stuffy, but I needed to know about Babington. "And Sir Anthony?" I asked.

"Calm and almost dignified," said Kathryn, "as befits a true-born gentleman. Which he was," she snapped, "whatever he has done since!"

"He was still alive when his innards were cut out," said Edmund. "I heard him say, 'Parce mihi.'"

"What does that mean, Kathryn?" I asked, knowing she has no Latin. "Oh, I remember, it means, 'Spare me.'"

She flushed, then glanced over my shoulder, as Joseph entered.

"Joseph!" cried Edmund. "We have been telling of the executions."

"I have heard," said Joseph. "It was brutal." He looked green.

Just then, Father came in and sat at the table, his head in his hands. "A bad business," he muttered. "What is she thinking of?"

When he realized Edmund and Kathryn were there, he smiled and became his usual self. But I knew he was pretending. I was right, for when they'd gone, he sagged again. "It was a bad business, Tilly," he said. "Those men were killed most brutally – at the Queen's wish. Lord, even the ordinary people are sickened by it. I pray that tomorrow will not be another day like this."

21st September 1586

Father's prayer was answered. Queen Elizabeth was so frightened and angered by the plot against her that she ordered the conspirators to suffer as much agony as possible. The executioners were told to ensure the traitors were still conscious when they were bowelled. But she has relented. Today's seven terrified victims were allowed to hang until they were dead, or at least unconscious.

Now they are gone. I do not want to think of Babington ever again.

5th October 1586

Father is to accompany Sir Francis Walsingham and the Queen's commissioners to Fotheringhay Castle, where Mary Stuart has been sent to stand trial for treason. Mother made him promise to remember everything. I suggested he might keep a diary, and he laughed. "If I had the days of leisure you two have," he said, "I might."

I wish I had fewer days of leisure. Imagine being a man, doing exciting, important things. Though not all have exciting lives – my poor Joseph finds everything a struggle.

26th October 1586

Father is home, the commissioners have met at Westminster, and the Scottish queen has been pronounced guilty of, as Father says, "compassing, practising and imagining of Her Majesty's death". Her fate is in Queen Elizabeth's hands. Sir Francis, of course, wishes for her death. He says the throne of England will not be safe until the Catholic threat is removed. He means Mary Stuart and, in his belief – and Father's – the Scottish queen must die.

27th October 1586

Poor Joseph has been in a deep gloom ever since the Babington affair, and he dreads restarting his studies.

"Kitty, I am not like Richard," he said, as we walked Pawpaw by the river. "When we were born, he got all the cleverness. I was left with little brain."

"Joseph, what you lack in brain, you make up for in sweetness of nature," I told him.

He smiled his gentle smile. "But what can I do? How can I tell Father all the money he spends on my education is wasted ... that I would be better off being a – a – a saddler, or a blacksmith."

Of course, he cannot tell Father that.

28th October 1586

What a day. Oh, *what* a day.

This morning, Father knocked on my door and told me to dress in my finest. "We are summoned to Sir Francis Walsingham's office at Greenwich Palace," he said. "Tom will bring the carriage round at midday."

I was completely flustered, but then Joseph burst into my chamber and grabbed me by the shoulders. I could not understand a word at first.

"Stop jabbering!" I forced him to sit down. "Be calm."

His breathing slowed and soon he could speak clearly enough for me to understand.

"Sir Francis, he wants me there so he can arrest me..."

"Joseph, you dear fool," I said, "if he wanted to arrest you, he would send men here. It cannot be that. Maybe he is returning Father's hospitality."

"In his office?"

He had a point. But Joseph need not have feared. Not for one moment. By the time we had reached Greenwich, drunk a welcome cup of wine and been shown to Sir Francis's office, we were all (except Father) open-mouthed at such grandeur.

Sir Francis was waiting with Richard. He welcomed Father, kissed Mother's hand, then turned to me and Joseph. "Ah, my two young friends." He kissed my hand and clasped Joseph's, beaming all the while. Then he excused himself and left the room.

Richard was whispering to Father and Mother, so I turned to Joseph and said, "Do you still think he will arrest you, pudding-head?"

But before he could reply, the door opened and in swept – Queen Elizabeth!

"Sir Nicholas, we meet again," she said, as Father bowed. I sank down into a curtsy so deep I almost sat on the floor.

The Queen turned to Mother, and raised her from her curtsy. "Lady Matilda," she said. "Tilly Middleton! How well we remember you the night you served us so well."

She says "we" and "us" instead of "I" and "me"! Very confusing.

"Do you still use our gifts?" the Queen continued.

"Every day of my life, Your Majesty," said Mother.

"Then perhaps you will also use this token of our regard for your family." The Queen pressed something into my mother's hand. Then she turned to Joseph.

"Another loyal Lumsden! Your brother, Richard, serves us well, and it is easy to see you are his twin." Joseph bowed, quite nicely. "We understand that you have had a brush with deceit and dishonour, and have emerged with your own honour intact. Tell me, would you serve us, too?"

Oh, Joseph was so embarrassing! He mumbled and stumbled, and bobbed little bows, and behind him I could see Sir Francis's eyes actually twinkling – not something I have seen before!

And then Her Majesty took my hand in her own! "Catherine Lumsden. You are a member of a family that has proved truly loyal to the crown. We must make sure that, when the time comes, you marry another loyal Englishman, so that your children continue the family tradition. Yes?"

"Yes, Your Majesty," I said. Actually, I don't like the thought of getting married at all, but you do not argue with the Queen.

Suddenly, she was gone!

And now we are home. I am so proud that my Father's service to his queen – although we still don't know exactly what he does – is so valued by her that she wished to honour his family. For honoured we are, Father says. He is to be given a large house in the country, Mother has on her second finger a ring with an emerald the size of a hazelnut (that was the Queen's token), I am to have the Queen's interest in my marriage (Mother is thrilled, though I am not), and – best of all – Joseph will leave Lincoln's Inn. He is to become Sir Francis Walsingham's special messenger – a job he can do well.

I have almost filled my book. Maybe the Queen will send me a diary on my birthday. But first, I must find a way to let her know when it is…

Historical Note

Elizabeth I was the daughter of Henry VIII and his second wife, Anne Boleyn.

When Henry couldn't persuade the Pope to agree to an annulment of his first marriage to Catherine of Aragon, he broke away from the Roman Catholic church, and established the Church of England. As he also made himself Supreme Head of the new church, he was able to arrange matters to suit himself. He divorced Catherine and married Anne.

When Henry died he was succeeded by Edward VI, his son by his third wife, Jane Seymour. Edward was a staunch Protestant who provided churches with Bibles in the English language so that all the people could understand it, and he declared that the Roman Catholic Latin church service was illegal.

Edward died while still in his teens, and was succeeded briefly by the Protestant Lady Jane Grey, and then by his half-sister, Mary Tudor. She was the daughter of Catherine of Aragon, and was a devout Catholic. Mary restored England to the Roman

Catholic church, and set about trying to stamp out Protestantism. She burned alive many people who might stand against her, and even imprisoned her Protestant half-sister, Princess Elizabeth, for a time, believing her to be a threat. Her severity earned her the nickname Bloody Mary. Many people wanted an end to Mary's reign, and Elizabeth, as her obvious successor, was a focus for Protestant plots.

In 1558, Mary Tudor died, and the throne passed to Elizabeth. At first hers was a more tolerant reign. As long as Catholics made no attempt to force their religion on her people, they were allowed to go about their lives in peace. There were so many Catholic plots, however, that Elizabeth became afraid for her life. She was forced to become tougher, making it illegal for priests to be in England, and for ordinary people to help or hide priests. Those who refused to attend the English, or Anglican, church were charged huge monthly fines – well over £3,000 in today's money.

Mary, Queen of Scots was a constant worry. While she lived, she was a focus for those who were intent on restoring the country to Roman Catholicism. If Elizabeth could be removed, and Mary put on the English throne, their ambitions would succeed.

The anti-Catholic Sir Francis Walsingham was constantly on the lookout for such plots, and formed a great network of spies both in England and abroad. It was well known that plotters would depend on help from an invading force, and his "ears" in other countries soon learned of invasion plans.

Thanks to such loyal servants, many plots were exposed, but all the time Walsingham knew that they would not stop until Mary, Queen of Scots was dead. Elizabeth was unwilling to harm her own cousin – a fellow queen – so Walsingham knew that Mary had to be implicated in a plot beyond a shadow of doubt if she was ever to be convicted and executed.

The Babington plot gave Walsingham just what he needed: letters to and from Mary, showing that she approved of a scheme to assassinate Elizabeth, and of Babington's plan to put her on the throne of England. Walsingham set a trap for Mary, and eventually succeeded in bringing her to trial.

In October 1586, Mary conducted her own defence in the Great Hall at Fotheringhay Castle, and protested her innocence throughout the two days of the trial.

For four months, Elizabeth couldn't bring herself to sign the warrant for her cousin's execution. Finally, in February 1587, she was persuaded to. Even then, she called back William Davison, the secretary who had taken the warrant, to ask if perhaps the matter might be dealt with by someone else. She didn't want to be the one responsible for Mary's death, and would rather the lady was quietly murdered.

But the warrant was delivered to Fotheringhay and, on 8 February, Mary was taken once again to the Great Hall, this time to face her executioner. She died bravely, with the words "Into your hands, O Lord" on her lips. When men came to remove her body, Mary's faithful little dog was found hiding beneath her skirts.

As soon as Elizabeth heard the news of the execution, she flew into a violent rage, swearing that she had never meant the warrant to be sent. Others had to take the blame. William Davison was sent to the Tower of London, and the Lord Treasurer banished from her presence.

With the Catholic queen dead and buried, the Protestant population could feel that the English throne was safer than it had ever been. But the death of Mary, Queen of Scots was always to weigh heavily on the mind of Queen Elizabeth.

Timeline

11 June 1509 Henry VIII marries Catherine of Aragon, the widow of his brother, at Greenwich.
18 February 1516 Henry and Catherine's daughter, Princess Mary, is born.
1527 Henry asks the Pope, in Rome, to annul his marriage to Catherine of Aragon.
11 February 1531 Henry VIII declares himself head of the Church of England.
January 1533 Henry and Anne Boleyn marry in a secret ceremony.
7 September 1533 Birth of Henry and Anne's daughter, Princess Elizabeth, at Greenwich Palace.
19 May 1536 Anne Boleyn is executed at the Tower of London.
Henry marries Jane Seymour.
1537 Jane Seymour gives birth to Prince Edward.
8 December 1542 Mary Stuart is born. Within a week, she becomes Queen of Scots.
1547 Death of Henry VIII.
Prince Edward becomes King Edward VI.

1548 Mary Stuart moves to France.

1553 Death of Edward VI.

Henry's daughter, Mary Tudor, becomes queen.

1555 Queen Mary begins persecuting Protestants in earnest.

1558 Death of Queen Mary.

Princess Elizabeth becomes queen.

Mary Stuart marries the Dauphin of France, the future Francis II.

1560 Francis dies, leaving Mary a widow.

1561 Mary returns to Scotland.

Anthony Babington is born, the third son of a wealthy Derbyshire family.

1565 Mary marries Lord Darnley.

1566 Mary gives birth to a son, the future King James VI of Scotland and James I of England.

1567 Murder of Lord Darnley.

Mary marries the Earl of Bothwell, who was involved in Darnley's murder.

Mary is imprisoned by her own people and forced to abdicate in favour of her son.

1568 Mary flees Scotland and arrives in England, seeking protection from Queen Elizabeth, but is imprisoned.

1570 Mary receives the Pope's support in her claim for the English throne.

Queen Elizabeth is excommunicated by the Pope.

1571 Discovery of the Ridolfi Plot to free Mary Stuart, marry her to the Duke of Norfolk, put her on the throne, and to restore Catholicism to England.

1572 The Duke of Norfolk is executed.

1577 Anthony Babington serves in the household of the Earl of Shrewsbury, where Mary Stuart is imprisoned.

1579 Babington marries Margaret (or Margery) Draycot.

1580 Babington is studying law in Lincoln's Inn, London.

Babington goes to France for several months.

Edmund Campion, a Jesuit priest, arrives in England.

1581 People can be fined £20 a month for not going to church.

Campion is accused of conspiring to overthrow Queen Elizabeth, and is executed.

Any Catholic priest discovered can be executed, by law.

1583 Discovery of the Throckmorton plot to overthrow Queen Elizabeth in favour of Mary Stuart.

1584 Spanish ambassador, Bernardino de Mendoza, is accused of involvement in the Throckmorton plot, and expelled from England.

William, Prince of Orange is assassinated.

1585 Anthony Babington travels overseas for several months.
1586 The Babington plot, which implicated Mary Stuart, is discovered.
September 1586 The conspirators in the Babington plot are executed.
October 1586 Mary is taken to Fotheringhay Castle and tried for treason.
1 February 1587 Queen Elizabeth signs Mary Stuart's death warrant.
8 February 1587 Mary, Queen of Scots, is executed.
1603 Queen Elizabeth dies, and is succeeded by James I of England and VI of Scotland, the son of Mary, Queen of Scots.

Picture acknowledgments

P 206 (top left)	The Art Archive/Musée du Château de Versailles/ Dagli Orti
P 206 (top right)	The Art Archive/Victoria and Albert Museum London/ Sally Chappell
P 206 (bottom)	Mary Evans Picture Library
P 207 (top)	Topham Picturepoint
P 207 (bottom)	Topham Picturepoint
P 208 (top)	Bridgeman Art Library/Private Collection
P 208 (bottom)	The Art Archive

The young Mary, Queen of Scots.

A portrait of Queen Elizabeth I.

Sir Francis Walsingham, Queen Elizabeth's Secretary of State.

A view of London Bridge and the City of London.

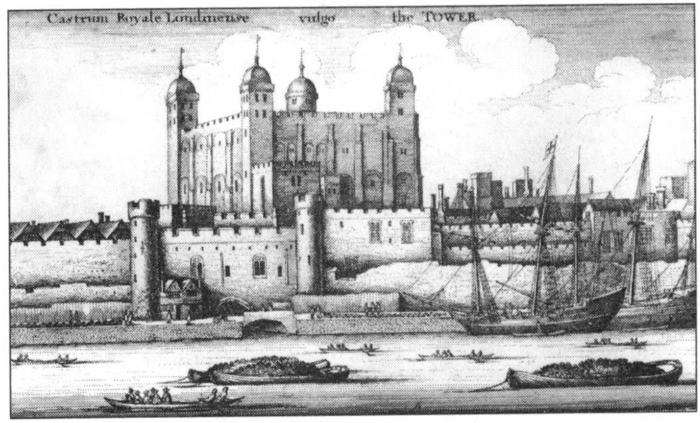

The Tower of London and the River Thames.

A drawing of Sir Anthony Babington and his co-conspirators.

A contemporary illustration showing the execution of Mary, Queen of Scots.